NO PITY

(A Valerie Law FBI Suspense Thriller —Book Two)

BLAKE PIERCE

Blake Pierce

Blake Pierce is the USA Today bestselling author of the RILEY PAGE mystery series, which includes seventeen books. Blake Pierce is also the author of the MACKENZIE WHITE mystery series, comprising fourteen books; of the AVERY BLACK mystery series, comprising six books; of the KERI LOCKE mystery series, comprising five books; of the MAKING OF RILEY PAIGE mystery series, comprising six books; of the KATE WISE mystery series, comprising seven books; of the CHLOE FINE psychological suspense mystery, comprising six books; of the JESSE HUNT psychological suspense thriller series, comprising twenty four books; of the AU PAIR psychological suspense thriller series, comprising three books; of the ZOE PRIME mystery series, comprising six books; of the ADELE SHARP mystery series, comprising fifteen books, of the EUROPEAN VOYAGE cozy mystery series, comprising four books; of the new LAURA FROST FBI suspense thriller, comprising nine books (and counting); of the new ELLA DARK FBI suspense thriller, comprising eleven books (and counting); of the A YEAR IN EUROPE cozy mystery series, comprising nine books, of the AVA GOLD mystery series, comprising six books (and counting); of the RACHEL GIFT mystery series, comprising six books (and counting); of the VALERIE LAW mystery series, comprising six books (and counting); of the PAIGE KING mystery series, comprising six books (and counting); and of the MAY MOORE mystery series, comprising three books (and counting).

An avid reader and lifelong fan of the mystery and thriller genres, Blake loves to hear from you, so please feel free to visit www.blakepierceauthor.com to learn more and stay in touch.

BOOKS BY BLAKE PIERCE

MAY MOORE MYSTERY SERIES
NEVER RUN (Book #1)
NEVER TELL (Book #2)
NEVER LIVE (Book #3)

PAIGE KING MYSTERY SERIES
THE GIRL HE PINED (Book #1)
THE GIRL HE CHOSE (Book #2)
THE GIRL HE TOOK (Book #3)
THE GIRL HE WISHED (Book #4)
THE GIRL HE CROWNED (Book #5)
THE GIRL HE WATCHED (Book #6)

VALERIE LAW MYSTERY SERIES
NO MERCY (Book #1)
NO PITY (Book #2)
NO FEAR (Book #3)
NO SLEEP (Book #4)
NO QUARTER (Book #5)
NO CHANCE (Book #6)

RACHEL GIFT MYSTERY SERIES
HER LAST WISH (Book #1)
HER LAST CHANCE (Book #2)
HER LAST HOPE (Book #3)
HER LAST FEAR (Book #4)
HER LAST CHOICE (Book #5)
HER LAST BREATH (Book #6)

AVA GOLD MYSTERY SERIES
CITY OF PREY (Book #1)
CITY OF FEAR (Book #2)
CITY OF BONES (Book #3)
CITY OF GHOSTS (Book #4)

CITY OF DEATH (Book #5)
CITY OF VICE (Book #6)

A YEAR IN EUROPE
A MURDER IN PARIS (Book #1)
DEATH IN FLORENCE (Book #2)
VENGEANCE IN VIENNA (Book #3)
A FATALITY IN SPAIN (Book #4)

ELLA DARK FBI SUSPENSE THRILLER
GIRL, ALONE (Book #1)
GIRL, TAKEN (Book #2)
GIRL, HUNTED (Book #3)
GIRL, SILENCED (Book #4)
GIRL, VANISHED (Book 5)
GIRL ERASED (Book #6)
GIRL, FORSAKEN (Book #7)
GIRL, TRAPPED (Book #8)
GIRL, EXPENDABLE (Book #9)
GIRL, ESCAPED (Book #10)
GIRL, HIS (Book #11)

LAURA FROST FBI SUSPENSE THRILLER
ALREADY GONE (Book #1)
ALREADY SEEN (Book #2)
ALREADY TRAPPED (Book #3)
ALREADY MISSING (Book #4)
ALREADY DEAD (Book #5)
ALREADY TAKEN (Book #6)
ALREADY CHOSEN (Book #7)
ALREADY LOST (Book #8)
ALREADY HIS (Book #9)

EUROPEAN VOYAGE COZY MYSTERY SERIES
MURDER (AND BAKLAVA) (Book #1)
DEATH (AND APPLE STRUDEL) (Book #2)
CRIME (AND LAGER) (Book #3)
MISFORTUNE (AND GOUDA) (Book #4)
CALAMITY (AND A DANISH) (Book #5)

MAYHEM (AND HERRING) (Book #6)

ADELE SHARP MYSTERY SERIES
LEFT TO DIE (Book #1)
LEFT TO RUN (Book #2)
LEFT TO HIDE (Book #3)
LEFT TO KILL (Book #4)
LEFT TO MURDER (Book #5)
LEFT TO ENVY (Book #6)
LEFT TO LAPSE (Book #7)
LEFT TO VANISH (Book #8)
LEFT TO HUNT (Book #9)
LEFT TO FEAR (Book #10)
LEFT TO PREY (Book #11)
LEFT TO LURE (Book #12)
LEFT TO CRAVE (Book #13)
LEFT TO LOATHE (Book #14)
LEFT TO HARM (Book #15)

THE AU PAIR SERIES
ALMOST GONE (Book#1)
ALMOST LOST (Book #2)
ALMOST DEAD (Book #3)

ZOE PRIME MYSTERY SERIES
FACE OF DEATH (Book#1)
FACE OF MURDER (Book #2)
FACE OF FEAR (Book #3)
FACE OF MADNESS (Book #4)
FACE OF FURY (Book #5)
FACE OF DARKNESS (Book #6)

A JESSIE HUNT PSYCHOLOGICAL SUSPENSE SERIES
THE PERFECT WIFE (Book #1)
THE PERFECT BLOCK (Book #2)
THE PERFECT HOUSE (Book #3)
THE PERFECT SMILE (Book #4)
THE PERFECT LIE (Book #5)
THE PERFECT LOOK (Book #6)

THE PERFECT AFFAIR (Book #7)
THE PERFECT ALIBI (Book #8)
THE PERFECT NEIGHBOR (Book #9)
THE PERFECT DISGUISE (Book #10)
THE PERFECT SECRET (Book #11)
THE PERFECT FAÇADE (Book #12)
THE PERFECT IMPRESSION (Book #13)
THE PERFECT DECEIT (Book #14)
THE PERFECT MISTRESS (Book #15)
THE PERFECT IMAGE (Book #16)
THE PERFECT VEIL (Book #17)
THE PERFECT INDISCRETION (Book #18)
THE PERFECT RUMOR (Book #19)
THE PERFECT COUPLE (Book #20)
THE PERFECT MURDER (Book #21)
THE PERFECT HUSBAND (Book #22)
THE PERFECT SCANDAL (Book #23)
THE PERFECT MASK (Book #24)

CHLOE FINE PSYCHOLOGICAL SUSPENSE SERIES
NEXT DOOR (Book #1)
A NEIGHBOR'S LIE (Book #2)
CUL DE SAC (Book #3)
SILENT NEIGHBOR (Book #4)
HOMECOMING (Book #5)
TINTED WINDOWS (Book #6)

KATE WISE MYSTERY SERIES
IF SHE KNEW (Book #1)
IF SHE SAW (Book #2)
IF SHE RAN (Book #3)
IF SHE HID (Book #4)
IF SHE FLED (Book #5)
IF SHE FEARED (Book #6)
IF SHE HEARD (Book #7)

THE MAKING OF RILEY PAIGE SERIES
WATCHING (Book #1)

WAITING (Book #2)
LURING (Book #3)
TAKING (Book #4)
STALKING (Book #5)
KILLING (Book #6)

RILEY PAIGE MYSTERY SERIES
ONCE GONE (Book #1)
ONCE TAKEN (Book #2)
ONCE CRAVED (Book #3)
ONCE LURED (Book #4)
ONCE HUNTED (Book #5)
ONCE PINED (Book #6)
ONCE FORSAKEN (Book #7)
ONCE COLD (Book #8)
ONCE STALKED (Book #9)
ONCE LOST (Book #10)
ONCE BURIED (Book #11)
ONCE BOUND (Book #12)
ONCE TRAPPED (Book #13)
ONCE DORMANT (Book #14)
ONCE SHUNNED (Book #15)
ONCE MISSED (Book #16)
ONCE CHOSEN (Book #17)

MACKENZIE WHITE MYSTERY SERIES
BEFORE HE KILLS (Book #1)
BEFORE HE SEES (Book #2)
BEFORE HE COVETS (Book #3)
BEFORE HE TAKES (Book #4)
BEFORE HE NEEDS (Book #5)
BEFORE HE FEELS (Book #6)
BEFORE HE SINS (Book #7)
BEFORE HE HUNTS (Book #8)
BEFORE HE PREYS (Book #9)
BEFORE HE LONGS (Book #10)
BEFORE HE LAPSES (Book #11)
BEFORE HE ENVIES (Book #12)
BEFORE HE STALKS (Book #13)

BEFORE HE HARMS (Book #14)

AVERY BLACK MYSTERY SERIES
CAUSE TO KILL (Book #1)
CAUSE TO RUN (Book #2)
CAUSE TO HIDE (Book #3)
CAUSE TO FEAR (Book #4)
CAUSE TO SAVE (Book #5)
CAUSE TO DREAD (Book #6)

KERI LOCKE MYSTERY SERIES
A TRACE OF DEATH (Book #1)
A TRACE OF MURDER (Book #2)
A TRACE OF VICE (Book #3)
A TRACE OF CRIME (Book #4)
A TRACE OF HOPE (Book #5)

PROLOGUE

A dark shape moved between the pine trees. The sight of it made Fred Maxwell's seventy-two-year-old heart thud in his chest.

There was something unnerving about that shape, moving slowly between the dense maple trees that dimmed the bright sun above to a whisper.

Fred suddenly felt very alone out there in the vast forest. For the first time in his life, he felt that his hobby of solitary camping was a dangerous one.

He stayed perfectly still in a small clearing in case it noticed him. Could it be a bear?

A human?

Fred hadn't expected to encounter another human. He was off the beaten path, no trail in sight. The nearest campsite was Greenwood Point, and that was at least a forty-minute hike from where he was.

The shape in the woods now changed. It crouched down further and went on all fours, moving over something in the ground. Fred couldn't be sure, but he thought he could just about make out the outline of a head taking in its surroundings.

He didn't dare move.

The shape's arms were moving, the elbows moving back and forth as the hands grasped at the large white object.

Fred stiffened, feeling sure it was a person.

But what the hell was it doing?

He could feel his own breath moving shakily, in and out.

He didn't know why he was so nervous—until the answer came to him: the stench of blood filled the air.

Fred did his best to push his dark suspicions—and that smell—to the back of his mind. But they sat there like a thorn.

The shape suddenly stood up tall and powerful and looked around, scanning the thick woodland.

Fred could feel his heart racing as he realized his life was in danger. He could feel a vein in his neck pushing forward as if ready to pop.

But, to his immense relief, the figure moved off, slowly at first, between the trees, swallowed up into anonymity by the deep green.

Fred approached slowly, warily, and he could see, on the ground, a torn shirt revealing white skin beneath.

A young woman.

She wasn't moving, nor would she ever again. There was too much blood for that.

As his mind grasped what lay before him, Fred let out a cry of revulsion and utter shock; one that echoed through the forest, deep between the woods and, no doubt, to the killer, now long disappeared.

CHAPTER ONE

Valerie followed the nurse through the sterile white corridors, her mind filled with worry for her sister. Suzie's condition was worsening and, no matter how hard she tried, Valerie felt like she was losing the battle for her sister's sanity.

This was the ninth time Valerie had visited her sister at Ealing Psychiatric Hospital. Each time she dreaded it more than the last. She hated everything about it, the two-hour drive from Quantico first thing in the morning, the nausea building in her stomach as each mile passed.

When she had seen the road sign to take the last exit off the highway that morning, Valerie thought about just driving on.

Valerie's main concern was for her sister's well-being, but the fear of watching her decline mentally was at times too hard to take. She kept thinking about that smiling, happy kid she remembered growing up, and how their mother's actions had eroded that sweet soul.

The urge to put as much distance between her and her family's past history of severe mental illness wasn't new. But she had come to see it as futile.

You can't outrun your past, her boyfriend, Tom, had told her. Now she knew he was right. The Harlow case a couple of months earlier had taught her that. The two brothers had been stained by a lifetime of torment, so much so that they both became killers in their own way, fractured right down to the center. Running from the past hadn't just proven futile for them, it had twisted them into violence and hatred.

Yes, running from her family was futile, but it didn't stop the occasional desire to keep trying. It was a desire she had to fight tooth and nail each time she headed out to visit her little sister, Suzie. How she loved her sister, and how helpless she felt in trying to protect her from her demons.

On this day, the staff at Ealing Psychiatric Hospital had been their usual selves, a mix of nurses and doctors, some with excellent people skills, others so deadened by their experiences that their bedside manners had seemingly been snuffed out.

As an FBI profiler hunting down the most depraved killers in the country, Valerie could sympathize with a need for emotional distance. But she could never give in to that need. She always felt the profound impact those killers had on countless families across the US. She bore that weight each and every day.

As Valerie was led through the hospital, back into the secure ward where her sister was being kept, she wondered what side of her sibling she would see today. Would she speak? Would she be angry? Would she grow violent?

Valerie was worried by how unpredictable her sister's behavior had become, and how much medication was now required to keep her on a more even keel. She was spiraling, and Valerie knew it.

"I'll be out here if you need me," the nurse said as she unlocked the metal door to Suzie's room. The lock clanked as it opened, prison-like and cold.

Valerie nodded to the nurse.

On-duty nurses always asked Valerie if she needed an orderly to be present for her own safety. But given the sensitive nature of her and her sister's conversations, she always requested privacy.

Valerie stepped into the room, the walls and ceiling sterile white, padding upon them. A cold light shone down from a caged light fitting above, put there to stop patients from breaking the bulb and cutting themselves.

A slight electric buzz came from it, reminding Valerie of the buzzing fly zappers placed in buildings to kill infestations.

She hated to see Suzie in such a place, but in the depths of her soul, Valerie truly feared something much worse—her own mind. With her mother and sister both committed, was it only a matter of time before her own instabilities showed?

That thought ate away at Valerie each night before falling asleep, and it often pursued her even through the waking day.

Suzie was wearing a white hospital gown, sitting at the end of her bed. She was looking at the ground. Her bare feet were placed firmly against the floor, and her blonde hair obscured her features.

Looking at her, Valerie would have been able to spot her sister from a mile away even if she couldn't see her face. It was the way she was sitting. Valerie remembered as a child, seeing Suzie sitting on the edge of her bed with the same posture, looking down at the ground as if she hoped it would swallow her up.

When they were children, Suzie had been the bright spark of the family. Always enthusiastic, always fun. But after their mother's psychotic breakdown, something had broken inside of her.

She had been in and out of psychiatric wards several times throughout her life, but these last couple of months were different.

Valerie knew it.

She wanted to protect her sister like she'd done when they were kids. Like she had done the night her mom had brandished that knife, spouting delusions about wanting to cut out the bad from them.

Valerie had stepped forward to protect Suzie that night more than twenty years before.

And she had the scars on her arms to prove it.

She wished she could do the same again, to take on the scars of her sister's mind, but that wasn't possible. It was a faceless enemy as insidious as anything on Earth.

There was now a silence in the sterile white room, not even disturbed by the occasional buzz of the light, almost as if it had been hushed by the tension.

It was time to start the conversation. The same one the two sisters had now had nine times.

"Suzie, it's Val."

Suzie didn't look up. She didn't stir.

To Valerie it was as if her sister had become a statue, frozen in the posture of her childhood, even though now she was a grown adult.

Valerie waited for a moment. During her visits, she had noticed conflict within herself. Part of her reacted as a family member, feeling emotive, reaching for the same questions, the same solutions as always, in desperation. But the other part of her belonged to the FBI. Having dealt with over a hundred mentally disturbed criminals, she found it difficult not to profile her own sister. No matter how hard she tried, her training now seemed as difficult to outrun as her past.

"Please, Suzie," Valerie said. "Talk to me."

Suzie moved. Her head rose a little. Her hands moved up off of the bed and parted the hair away from her face, resting its long strands behind her ears. Suzie's hands had a slow shake to them. Equally slow was her gaze as she finally looked at her older sister and locked gazes with her.

"They've upped your medication." Valerie could see it in her sluggish movements and almost vacant stare.

Suzie nodded. "Yeah."

"I'm sorry."

"They said I need to take a sedative to stop the angry outburst,"

5

Suzie continued, giving a sleepy grin. "I wouldn't get angry if they'd just let me out of here."

"You've got to do everything you can to stay stable, Suzie. It's the only way you're going to get out of here." This was more of a hope than an expectation for Valerie.

Suzie scoffed. "You don't get it, Val. You don't know what it's like staring at these walls all day. If I wasn't crazy before, I am now."

Valerie shook her head and sighed. "I just want you to get better. I want us to have a relationship outside of here."

"I know," said Suzie. "But maybe I wouldn't have ended up in here if my big sister hadn't abandoned me for years."

Those words stung Valerie.

Deep down, she knew they were true. For all her attempts to protect her sister over the years, Valerie had finally drifted away into her own life: a career, an apartment, a boyfriend. This had begun when Suzie had insisted on staying in touch with their mom, another resident of a different psychiatric hospital.

Valerie secretly worried about her own mental health, and in a desperate attempt to protect herself, she had pulled away from her little sister, wanting nothing to do with their mother and the pain of those memories.

"You know why I left, Suzie."

"Don't bring Mom into this, Val. Don't blame her because you were too weak to stick around."

Valerie was about to say something in return, but she swallowed the words. She didn't want to set her sister off. She wished Suzie could understand that their mother's violent moods when they were younger made a relationship impossible.

But that was the irony. Valerie had promised herself that she would *never* speak to her mother again. Now, though, the tables had turned.

"Is she still not seeing you?" asked Suzie. "She can spin on a dime, can't she?"

"The hospital contacts me," Valerie explained with agitation. "They say she's ready to talk, then I travel there and she refuses to see me. It's almost as if it's a game to her. Have me travel all the way out there, just to tell the orderlies to keep me out of her sight."

A scream sounded far off. For a moment, Valerie feared it was the voice of repressed anger rattling around inside her mind. But she soon realized it was one of the other patients. Screaming from a delusion or anger, the truth didn't matter. It was pained either way.

"This place…" Valerie whispered, wondering if she would be the next in line to end up committed.

"What was so important about those papers I gave you?" Suzie asked, seemingly immune to the sound of screaming patients. "She said she wanted to talk to you about them."

Their mother had sent papers to Suzie, specifically intended for Valerie. They seemed like nonsense to Suzie, but Valerie knew they had a deeper meaning. The papers had been a way for their mother to reach out to Valerie, dangling the carrot of some terrible revelation about their past.

Valerie was now, for the first time in years, willing to talk to her mom to find out more and to make sense of the papers. But suddenly, her mom had other ideas.

"Yes," Valerie answered. "But, like I said, she's changed her mind for some reason. She won't let me visit."

Suzie turned her head and glared at the shut door.

"Maybe she doesn't like being treated like a criminal."

"She is a criminal," Valerie said. Technically, it was true, but Valerie knew this was like a red rag to a bull for Suzie.

Suzie stood up. "How can you think that? She's ill!"

"It doesn't matter if you're ill," Valerie answered, thinking back to her mother standing over her with a knife in her hand, wide-eyed and spouting delusions about cutting the devil out of her daughters. "Most people who have mental health issues aren't violent."

"And so, what? Throw away the key? Leave your mom to rot like she was in control? And what about me?"

Suzie stepped forward and stared Valerie in the face.

"Do you want to keep me in here? Let me rot, too?"

"No," Valerie said. "You're a victim in all of this." Her heart sank at the sight of her sister.

Suzie began to twirl some strands of her own hair in her hand. Her eyes darted around the room nervously, as if she were afraid of something.

Valerie's training made itself known again.

She's about to have a break.

"Maybe if you could speak to Mom on the phone," Valerie offered, trying to steer her sister back to a stable place. "You could ask her to see me?"

But it was too late.

Suzie turned away from her sister and then ran to the door.

"Get this bitch out of here!" she screamed, her words breaking up.

"Suzie, please, if you'd just speak with Mom…"

Suzie started screaming. She dropped to her knees and then began wrenching clumps of hair out of her head.

"Suzie, no!" Valerie dropped down next to her sister and grabbed hold of her wrists.

Suzie's screams pierced Valerie's hearing.

"I hate you!" Suzie shouted as Valerie restrained her on the floor.

The door opened with force and two orderlies rushed in.

"She's trying to pull her hair out," Valerie tried to say. But she was drowned out by Suzie's screams as they restrained her to the bed.

The on-duty nurse rushed in with a syringe. And once Suzie was in restraints, her wrists and legs secured to the bed, the nurse injected her with a sedative.

Suzie struggled at first, but in moments she calmed. Her eyes were vacant, staring at the wall, her breathing now steady.

"You better leave, Ms. Law," the nurse said.

Valerie wanted to tell her sister that she loved her. But she was in shock. Instead, she was escorted from the room.

On the way back down the corridor out of the ward, the nurse tried to comfort Valerie. But there was no comfort in that place. None to be given or taken.

A scream sounded.

Just like the distant one Valerie had heard while talking to her sister. But she couldn't be sure this time if it was an anonymous patient or Suzie herself.

Leaving the ward behind, Valerie walked in almost a daze into the elevator, her emotions frazzled.

As the elevator descended to the ground floor, she tried to persuade herself that it would be okay. Her sister would get better. But deep down she knew this was uncertain, as was her own fate.

A series of psychotic breaks had ravaged her mother's life, and now her sister was following suit.

The doors pinged open into the lobby, and Valerie left the looming psychiatric building behind, wondering how long it would be until the sickness came for her.

Her phone answered the sound of the doors with its own ping. Valerie looked down and saw a photograph. It was from her boyfriend, Tom. He had taken a picture of two wine glasses.

"You, me, and some vino," the caption read.

Valerie would have looked forward to this, but she knew that Tom would ask her about her sister, and those questions were just a reminder of how bad things were. Especially when she didn't know the answers herself.

But Tom would ask them anyway. She looked at her watch. She had to get moving so she wouldn't be late.

CHAPTER TWO

The rain running down the back of Valerie's neck made her wince. She pulled out her keys at the apartment building door and quickly disappeared inside. The world had done enough to Valerie for the day; she wouldn't abide by its cruelty for longer than she needed.

She wasn't physically tired. World-weary would have been a better way to put it. Emotionally exhausted after her visit with Suzie.

In the lobby of her apartment building, she saw that the elevators were out. A sign read "out of order."

Great.

She trudged up several flights of stairs, looking forward to soaking in a hot bath, but as she walked along the carpeted hallways to her apartment, Valerie could smell pomodoro sauce.

Tom's here, she thought.

Two weeks earlier, she'd taken the biggest leap of her life in a relationship. She'd given him a key to her apartment. For some, this might have been a small step, but to Valerie, it was opening her world up to another person like never before. She'd increasingly kept people at arm's length, but Tom was moving in ever decreasing circles, getting closer inch by inch.

Her greatest fear was that he would be the first to see the family madness in her, that he would be exposed to it before she was even aware that it had taken root.

Valerie opened the door to her apartment and disappeared inside. The smell of cooking filled the air, and the sound of her Otis Redding records being butchered by Tom singing over them accompanied the scent.

"*Hold her, please her, squeeze her, ya gotta, ya gotta, try a little tenderness,*" Tom belted out over the steam from the stove, clearly unaware that Valerie was now staring at him from the kitchen doorway.

And what a sight he was.

He was wearing one of Valerie's kitchen aprons, singing into a wooden spoon as a pot bubbled up with pasta in it before him. Even in such a goofy situation, he cut a tall handsome figure as usual, his chiseled jaw and tousled brown hair alluring to Valerie.

He wasn't wearing his glasses, making him seem less bookish than he actually was beneath that athletic exterior.

Tom suddenly turned and saw her, embarrassment etched on his face.

"Is there any chance you didn't see that?" he said, putting the wooden spoon into the pot.

Valerie laughed. Tom's good nature was exactly what she needed. It wouldn't cure her worries, but it could soothe them. She walked over and gave him a peck on the mouth.

"Next time you want to murder a classic song, pick someone other than Otis, okay?"

Tom laughed and nodded. He looked into Valerie's eyes.

"How did the visit go with Suzie?"

Valerie shook her head.

"No good. She's getting worse."

"I'm so sorry, Val," said Tom. "Maybe she's just having a dip and she'll bounce back."

"I hope so." Valerie turned to the nearest kitchen cupboard, retrieved a wine glass, and then poured herself a glass of red wine Tom had already opened.

"Do you think she'll help you speak to your mom?"

"I doubt it…" said Valerie, taking a sip of the wine. "She's in the dark as much as I am. I just don't get it. Why would Mom go to all that trouble to see me, to give Suzie those messages for me, only to refuse at the last moment when I turned up?"

Tom sighed in sympathy, but this was diluted by a brooding frustrating beneath. The question Valerie had asked had been put to him several times over the previous weeks.

"Well, maybe if you told me what your mom's message said in those papers Suzie gave you… maybe I could help?"

Valerie had thought about sharing everything with Tom. She wanted to tell him. She ached to share her fears. Several weeks earlier, Suzie had given her pieces of paper with her mother's scribbled handwriting all over it.

Suzie couldn't make heads or tails of it. But Valerie could. Her mind was a funnel for detection, a filter that let her remove the superfluous to get at a problem's true meaning.

But the meaning of her mom's message was too horrifying to share.

Valerie needed to know the truth behind it before she told anyone else. The consequences would have been disastrous for both her personal and professional life if the message were true.

Just as Tom rolled his eyes a little at being shut out from the truth yet again, Valerie's phone sprang to life.

"Saved by the bell," she said, picking up her phone and answering it. "Hi, Boss."

On the other end was Jackson Weller.

Valerie knew immediately that something had happened, something bad. His tone was grave, and his words had an urgency to them that could only mean someone's life was on the line.

"I know this is your day off, Agent Law," he said.

"Why do I detect a 'but'?" she said with a wry smile.

"Two murders in the last few days have come across my desk," Jackson continued. "I'm certain this is the work of a serial killer. And…"

"You think there's going to be a third?"

"Yes." Jackson was always concise when time was not on their side. "It's the exact type of case the Criminal Psychopathy Unit was set up for.

"You think escalation?"

"I'd need you to figure that out at the scene. You're my best, Valerie. You, Charlie, and Dr. Cooper. I'd appreciate if you could look at it today and see if you can grab the rest of the team." Jackson always resorted to Valerie's first name when he really wanted something. A personal touch. Valerie was a sucker for that. After all, Jackson was the first boss she'd ever had who in her opinion really cared about his agents.

Valerie looked at the bubbling pasta next to her. Tom was already sighing again, turning the stove off. He mouthed the words *It's okay.*

"Okay, Boss," she said into the phone. "Can you send the deets over to my phone?"

"Of course," he said. "And head straight to the scene after getting Charlie, it's a bit of a drive. We'll debrief later."

"I'm on it."

Tom turned to Valerie as soon as the phone call ended.

"I take it I'm eating alone this evening?"

Valerie moved over to him and wrapped her arms around him. "Do I infuriate you?"

"Only forty-five percent of the time," Tom said, smiling. "I get it.

It's your job."

"Would you prefer I did something else?"

"No, I guess not," Tom said. "You wouldn't be you, Val, if you weren't out there trying to help people."

Valerie looked to the side. She reached over and grabbed the wooden spoon from one of the simmering pots. Touching the pomodoro sauce to her mouth, she tasted it.

"It would have been lovely," she said. "But I've got something to make up for it." She grabbed Tom's hand and led him into their bedroom.

"I thought you didn't have time?" Tom laughed.

"You should be so lucky," said Val. "Open that dresser over there."

Tom stepped over and opened the top drawer.

"It's empty."

"All those drawers are," she said. "I'm not saying I'm ready for us to move in together, Tom. But I do think you should have somewhere to put your things, just in case."

"Thanks, Val," he said. "I know commitment isn't exactly easy for you."

"I'm trying."

"Me too."

Valerie's phone bleeped out a notification. It was some of the details of the case.

"You better go," Tom said.

They kissed, and Valerie headed back out into the world. A world that had given her a reprieve, but only a small one. She looked at her phone as she headed into the rain toward her car.

Another killer, she thought. *There's always one nearby.*

CHAPTER THREE

Valerie stopped outside the house and listened. The voices inside were muffled, but they were laughing. Something was going on, but then it always was at Charlie's house.

Charlie had been her partner at the FBI for years, and over that time, Valerie had been made to feel like part of his family. Whenever she was around them, it was a welcome reprieve from the difficulties of her own.

The sound of kids enjoying themselves was a good antidote to the work she and Charlie had to deal with every day. She was glad he had that in his life, and sad that she did not.

Ringing the doorbell, Valerie waited for a brief moment. She felt bad to disturb their happiness, especially considering Charlie was supposed to be getting some downtime. But she needed him by her side if the case really was going to be as heavy as Jackson had made out on the phone. As the lead investigator on the team, it was her job to break the bad news, and she had decided to do it face to face for a change.

Valerie wondered for a moment why that was.

Just as she considered that she had come to Charlie's home rather than phoning so she could be reminded of what a healthy family felt like, footsteps sounded.

It was Angela, Charlie's wife, who opened the door.

Angela was beautiful, her long brown hair wavy to her shoulders. She was smart, too, having a PhD in sociology. Angela's other defining characteristic was her displeasure at seeing Valerie on her doorstep without some notice. She always knew that meant Charlie was about to leave for an extended period.

"Not today," she said, frowning.

"I'm afraid so, Angela," answered Valerie. "I'm sorry."

"We're just sitting down for dinner, have you eaten?" Angela asked, still shaking her head at the unannounced arrival.

"No," Valerie said, thinking back to Tom's uneaten pasta. "I don't think we'll have time."

"Aunty Valerie!" two young voices screamed with delight, running down the hallway.

"Oh no, two little monsters!" Valerie laughed, opening her arms and embracing the children.

Little Georgina and Richard were Charlie and Angela's kids. Georgina was only three, Richard, five, and throughout the years Valerie had become part of their lives.

"Charlie!" Angela yelled. "The other woman is here!" She liked to joke about that. Anyone else would have taken it the wrong way, but Valerie found it funny, though awkward.

"Don't shoot the messenger," Valerie said as Charlie appeared from around the corner chomping on a bit of salami. Charlie could be intimidating with his tall, muscular build, but when he smiled, his dark brown good looks and his kind eyes could put anyone at ease.

"Charlie!" Angela said with a scowl. "I'm just plating dinner."

"Sorry," he said with his mouth full. "I was hungry."

"I'm really sorry, Angela," Valerie offered. "I don't think he'll have time. Jackson wants us."

Angela sighed. "And what Jackson wants, Jackson gets, I suppose."

"Dad, do you have to go?" Richard asked, running up to his father.

Charlie picked up his son and gave him a hug. "Yeah, sorry, kiddo. There are baddies out there."

"Can't they wait? You promised we'd play."

"Then who would take care of the baddies?"

Richard looked at Valerie. "Aunt Val?"

"No one takes care of the baddies like your old man, Richard," Valerie said, trying not to sound sarcastic.

"I'll call as soon as I know how long I'm going to be, love you all," he said, giving Angela a peck on the cheek as he left.

"Make sure he eats something a little healthier, would you?" Angela asked Valerie.

"I'll do my best." Valerie gave the kids a hug and then stepped outside with Charlie.

The door closed.

"Baddies? You fight 'baddies'?" Valerie said with a smirk. "I haven't heard that since I was a kid."

"No, no," Charlie said as they walked. "We catch baddies. There's a difference. The kids are just at that age where they're fascinated by what we do. I obviously don't want to tell them the nitty-gritty. Catching baddies was about as well as I could do without scaring them."

15

A moment of silence fell between the two friends as they exited Charlie's front yard. It was like a palate cleanser. A need to leave happiness behind as they moved toward something much more grim.

"I hate when you go all silent on me," Charlie said, walking to Valerie's car. "I take it this is a bad case?"

Valerie had looked at the details Jackson had sent her. It had been a cursory glance, but it was enough to let her know they were in for a rough time of it.

Catching baddies, she thought. *I wish it were that simple.*

"Two women have been murdered in the last few days," Valerie explained. "The second murder happened earlier today at Washington and Jefferson National Forests."

"No debrief at HQ first?" Charlie asked, sounding puzzled.

"No," Valerie said, stopping at her car. "Jackson wants us to appraise the scene while it's still fresh. He thinks the two murders are connected. If they are, then we're dealing with an especially violent and twisted serial killer. It's why law enforcement needs our help profiling the perp."

"We better move quickly, then."

CHAPTER FOUR

Valerie knew Charlie wanted to drive. It always irked him whenever Valerie took the wheel. But Valerie had difficult things on her mind, and she knew the open road would at least focus it away from her personal troubles and toward the case at hand.

But it was a two-hour drive, and in that time, conversation inevitably twisted toward the personal, as the car twisted its own way through the gray afternoon.

"You know," said Charlie, "when I saw you at my house, I thought something bad had happened to you."

Valerie was surprised to hear this; she thought she hid her feelings well. But she guessed that when you knew someone as long as she'd known Charlie, you got to learn each other's poker tells. Either that or her social mask was slipping in a way she didn't quite comprehend yet.

"Nothing gets past you, Charlie."

"I like to think so," Charlie said with mock pride. "I am a federal agent after all."

"What does your training tell you?" Valerie asked, turning the wheel gently and heading off of the highway toward the countryside.

"Never mind my training." Charlie's tone had become more serious. "Look, don't get mad, but Tom told me you had some family issues going on. I don't want to pry, but…"

"You're going to anyway?" Valerie was irked. In recent weeks Tom and Charlie had become friends. To Valerie, it was like crossing the streams. She was able to keep the lid on her worries at work, and the last thing she needed was for Tom to start confiding her business to her work colleagues.

This was especially true in the FBI. Any sign that she was struggling with her mental health, and she'd be mothballed for the foreseeable. She knew implicitly that Charlie would never shop her to their superiors, but if her fears were real, if she was inevitably to experience the mental decline of her mother and sister before her, it would be Charlie who would pick up on it first.

"Look," Charlie said, stammering as he fumbled for the words to say, "I know it's none of my business, it's just that…"

"You're worried about me," said Valerie.

"Yeah," Charlie said, with a degree of relief in his voice. "And you're worried about your sister."

"How can you tell?" she asked, pushing the car into fifth gear and opening the throttle as the car sped down a country road, flanked on all sides by open fields.

"This is the first time I've seen you drive this fast," Charlie pointed out. "You must be agitated."

"I'm not agitated," Valerie said, her voice rising a pitch. "I'm just… stressed."

"I understand," said Charlie. "I just want to say, if there's anything I can do, please let me know."

"There's nothing you can do," said Valerie, her foot pushing the gas pedal to the floor. "No one can do anything."

There was a silence between them. The hum of the car engine wrestled against the road surface as a dark cloud above began to scatter rain all around.

Valerie's mind was racing. Tom didn't know everything about her sister and mother, but she had let him in to a degree. He'd even been to the psychiatric hospital once the first time she'd visited Suzie.

He didn't know everything. But of what did understand, how much had he told Charlie?

This worried Valerie greatly. She loved Charlie as one of her dearest friends, but he was still her work colleague.

She slowed down as she came to a junction. To the left was a sign for George Washington and Jefferson National Forests.

"What exactly did Tom tell you, Charlie?" The words escaped from her mouth without any restraint.

"Don't get mad at Tom, I had to practically squeeze it out of him," Charlie said as the car stopped at the junction. "Besides, I already knew you had a sister and you don't like to talk about her. Tom just told me she was ill and you were stretched thin trying to look out for her."

Valerie's pulse began to race. Did Charlie know why her sister was ill?

"What did Tom tell you about Suzie?" she asked quietly as she took the left turn at the junction.

"He said she…" Charlie began, and then he stopped. "He said she became ill, and you were looking after her. That was it, more or less."

"What else?" Valerie asked.

"He said you'd made some sort of discovery about your family recently, something about a message from your mom, and that it was putting a strain on you," Charlie said, warily. "But Tom clammed up after that. He wouldn't tell me anything else."

"Did he tell you why my sister is ill?"

"No. It's none of my business," Charlie offered. "But I just want you to know you can talk to me whenever you want."

That's right, Valerie thought. *My mother tried to cut up me and my sister during a psychotic episode and Suzie, my sister, is now suffering from violent psychosis. Oh, and I think I might end up there myself one day.*

But Valerie said none of this. The landscape opened up before her on the road, fields of dark green and yellow beneath a caustic sky.

"I'm sorry if I overstepped, Val," Charlie finally said.

"Don't be," she sighed, "it's not your fault. It's not anyone's fault. It's just there. It's always there... her condition, I mean. I just have some things I need to work through..."

Valerie pulled into the side of the road. It weaved away behind and in front into a clutch of trees and hills. Valerie put on the handbrake.

She turned to her partner.

"I need you to promise me something, Charlie."

"Anything."

"If you ever have worries about me..."

"Worries?" Charlie said, puzzled. "Like... about your state of mind?"

"I didn't say that," Valerie said. *He knows,* she thought. *He sees. There is something wrong with me.*

"You mean if you're stressed?" Charlie asked.

"Just..." Val paused for a moment, thinking how best to put it. "Just, if you ever have concerns about me. Anything at all. Don't go to Jackson, come to me first. Okay?"

Charlie nodded.

"Promise me."

Charlie raised his hand in a salute. "Scout's honor."

Valerie looked to the sprawling landscape ahead, put the car into Drive, and continued on.

"We'll be at the death scene soon," Valerie said, changing the subject. "But we're going to have to hike for a while before we get there."

"Hike?" Charlie inquired.

19

"Yeah," said Valerie. "It's off the beaten path."

Valerie drove deeper into the forest, the trees blotting out the gray light above. She steadied her thoughts and prepared herself for a brutal murder scene.

CHAPTER FIVE

Valerie's lungs were burning. She considered herself fit; she had to be for her line of work. But even still, the long hike up a steep incline into the woods from the nearest road had taken it out of her.

"That was tough," Charlie said.

Valerie nodded, but she knew he'd barely broken sweat with his military background.

"Here, drink some water," a voice said from between the maple trees up ahead.

"I just need to sit for a moment…" another voice answered.

Valerie and Charlie emerged through a line of trees to see their friend and colleague, Dr. Will Cooper, sitting on an overturned log. Standing over him was a park ranger, holding out a water bottle.

Will was not dressed for the outdoors, still in casual clothes with a distinctively professorial flair. But that was Will all over. He was one of the most well-respected experts in the field of profiling, though most of his experience had come from academia.

That had changed on their first case together just a couple of months previous. The Harlow case. Since then, Valerie and Charlie had come to see how important Will's insight was in understanding a killer's next move.

A bond was forming, and for Valerie, Will's greatest trait was that he was unflinchingly kind, supportive, and wise.

"You okay, Will?" Valerie asked as they approached.

"That hike damn near killed me," he replied.

"I'm impressed you got here, Doc," Charlie said. "That was a difficult trek."

"This kind ranger, Matthew here," Will said, wiping the sweat from his brow. "He got me through it."

"I'm Ranger Phillips," the man said, shaking Valerie's and then Charlie's hand.

"Nice to meet you," Valerie said, but her attention was trained on two points of interest. The first was a man in his seventies sitting with a blanket over him, being comforted by another ranger. The second point of interest was what had caused that man significant distress.

The exposed body of a young woman lay between two large maple trees on the forest floor.

"Is that the witness?" Charlie asked, pointing to the elderly man.

"Yes," Ranger Phillips answered. "His name's Fred Maxwell. We know him. A good man. Comes up here regularly. Damn shame he found what he did. It's really shaken him."

"Tell me, Ranger Phillips," asked Valerie. "Is there an easier way up here?"

"Not really," he replied. "Easier terrain, maybe, but much longer, out past Greenwood Point."

"What are you thinking?" Will asked, finally standing up.

"No roads up here at all?" Valerie continued with her questions.

The ranger shook his head.

"Any camping gear near the victim?"

Again the ranger shook his head.

"That's strange for such a remote location," Charlie mused.

"Are there many trails here?" Valerie asked.

"Not many in this part of the park," the ranger replied. "In fact, it's a miracle old Fred stumbled across this. If he hadn't been deliberately trying to stay away from other hikers and campers like he always does, he'd never have been here in a million years."

"So where's the nearest trail from here?" Valerie looked around her at the trees moving gently in the light breeze.

"There is one," the ranger answered. "The Crying Wolf trail. It's heavily overgrown, and there are rocks and other debris all about it. It provides a seriously difficult challenge. Most stay clear of it. It's about a quarter of a mile from here. But due to the incline and conditions, you'd have to be a serious hiker to tackle it. Still, she'd have to wander some from the trail to end up here."

Valerie rubbed her head for a moment and then said, quietly: "We have three possibilities, then. The victim was either lost, dragged here against her will, or came to meet someone deliberately."

Charlie looked up at the sky.

"We're losing daylight, we should do the evaluation quickly."

Valerie agreed, as did Will.

"Why don't I speak with the witness?" Charlie asked.

"Good idea," replied Valerie.

Charlie nodded, took out a notepad he used for interviews, and headed over toward Fred Maxwell.

"Will and I will look at the body. Ranger Phillips, please lead the way," said Valerie.

In only a few moments, they were standing over the hideous crime scene.

"Not a pretty sight," Will said, placing a hand to his mouth to stifle a gag.

"This is going to take a lot of work," Valerie noted, feeling utterly disgusted by what the killer had done. "The victim's body is in a very bad way. I've never seen anything like this. Her body has been broken open."

Will nodded grimly. "She looks like she's been mauled by an animal. Are we certain this is a homicide?"

"It is," Valerie said, taking out her phone and documenting the grisly remains.

"How can you be sure?" Will asked, looking appalled at the large gaping wounds all over the woman's body.

Valerie pointed to a piece of white rib bone sticking out from the woman's side.

"There's a small piece of metal embedded on the side of that bone."

Both Ranger Phillips and Will leaned in.

"Remarkable," Will said, "that you could spot such a small flake of metal so easily, Valerie."

Valerie didn't say anything. The horror of the victim's mauled body had infected Valerie's senses. The smell of blood mixed with the pine of the forest. This was no place to bask in compliments.

She tried not to look at the face of the victim, but that was the strangest aspect of the girl's murder to Valerie.

"Not a drop of blood on her face," Will observed, as though reading Valerie's mind.

"I've never seen anything like that before," she said.

"What, if you don't mind me asking?" said the ranger.

"Usually," Valerie explained, "the face is a prime target for the killer. This is especially true when the victim is a beautiful young woman as we have here. Most killers who murder so brutally disfigure the face as a mark of disrespect."

Will covered his mouth, trying not to gag. He leaned over the face of the woman.

"The killer," he added, "has cleaned the face. Look."

Valerie saw what Will was pointing at. A leaf on the floor of the forest next to the woman's right ear looked to Valerie as though it had been used to wipe blood away from the ear lobe.

"He wanted the face pristine," Valerie pondered aloud. "This isn't the first time he's killed."

"How can you tell that?" the ranger asked again.

"Because a first-time killer is hurried and haphazard," Will answered. "This killer has gone to the trouble of cleaning her face. It might seem like insanity, and it probably is, but there'll be a reason behind it. A motivation. That isn't always apparent with a first kill."

"Adrenaline takes over," Valerie said, standing up. "The killer gets carried away. But not this time… Wait a minute."

Valerie had spotted something underneath a large fern nearby. She moved over to it. Pushing a leaf out of the way, she revealed a dark green trail shoe.

"This must be the victim's," she said. "And look at the sole."

"Worn down," the ranger replied.

"She was either wearing secondhand shoes or she was an experienced hiker. Maybe she was tackling the Crying Wolf trail after all?"

"It's possible," the ranger replied. "If you guys don't mind, could you talk to old Fred? He's been out here for hours and I'd really like to get him somewhere warm before it gets dark."

Valerie and Will took one more mournful look at the poor woman on the forest floor, or what remained of her, and then walked over to Charlie, who was questioning the witness.

"Like a shadow," Fred said, rubbing the white stubble on his cheek. "Never seen anything like it in all my years camping."

"This is Fred Maxwell," Charlie said as Valerie and Will arrived with the ranger. "Fred, this is Agent Valerie Law and Doctor Will Cooper."

"Doctor!?" Fred said in a panicked voice. "I'm not getting put in a psych ward, am I?"

"Of course not," Will replied. "But why would you think such a thing, Mr. Maxwell?"

Fred shook his head. "Like I've been telling your friend Agent Carlson, here, I saw what I saw."

"Wait," Valerie said hopefully. "Mr. Maxwell, did you see the killer?"

"Saw him?" Fred said in disbelief. "The damned thing could have chased me down in a second I was so close."

"Thing?" asked Will.

"Well," said Fred, "I thought it was a man. Had the eyes of one, the shape, too. But he ran off fast. Like lightning. And when I saw what he'd done to that poor girl… Dear God…"

"I'm sorry you had to see such a thing," said Valerie. ""But I think we can be certain it was a person. You think a man?"

"Man or something worse," Fred said. "You hear stories about Bigfoot, never believed them. But maybe. I mean, how could a man do that with his bare hands?"

"He didn't," offered Will. "Agent Law found evidence of a knife."

Valerie was still occasionally shocked by Will. For all of his brilliance and experience interviewing serial killers, he wasn't well versed in the do's and don'ts of field work.

"Let's not share our findings with the public just yet," she said. "But yes, Mr. Maxwell, I think we can rule out Bigfoot. The murderer was a man."

"Do you know which direction he ran in?" Will asked.

"The way you came," Fred said quickly. "I can't do that route because of my knees, but I know it gets you out of here quicker than any other."

"So, he either came that way or knows the area," Valerie mused. "Mr. Maxwell, can you give us any description of the man, his height, build, that sort of thing?"

"Hard to say," answered Fred. "But he seemed tall. Difficult to tell in here when your nerves are shredded."

"I know it's been quite an ordeal," offered Valerie. "But would you mind accompanying Ranger Phillips to the local police station for a few more questions?"

Fred nodded, clearly tired.

"Thank you for your help, Mr. Maxwell," Valerie said. "And Ranger Phillips, can you have someone rendezvous with our forensics team and show them the Crying Wolf trail? Just in case there's any evidence the victim came from there."

"Sure thing."

Ranger Phillips helped the elderly camper to his feet and walked him off in another direction.

From a distance, Fred stopped for a moment, turned, and said: "I've been coming here for years. But I'll never be back. Not after this. A place gets stained after something like this." His voice quivered. "You please give that poor girl a good burial."

Fred then turned and continued with the ranger, finally disappearing from the woods he so loved.

"Charlie," Valerie said, turning to her partner, "can you call HQ to see how long the forensics and body retrieval will take?"

"Sure," said Charlie. He pulled out his phone and then looked over to the exposed body of the young woman. "I hope they're quick. She... She shouldn't be left like that."

"I know," Valerie said, patting Charlie on the arm.

"Jackson didn't tell me much over the phone," observed Will. "I take it there are other killings related to this one?"

"There was another killing a few days ago, Jackson thinks they're related."

Valerie looked up at the canopy above. The forest should have been a peaceful place.

"*The woods are lovely, dark and deep...*" she whispered quietly.

"*And I have promises to keep,*" Will answered. "Robert Frost? I had no idea you enjoyed poetry."

"That's just always stuck with me," said Valerie. "But I've always felt that the woods can be more than lovely. They can be hideous."

"How so?" asked Will.

Valerie pointed over to the victim. "It's a place for evil people to hide their worst works."

Valerie sat down on an old log, her back now to the grisly scene behind her. She waited for the forensics team, hoping they would find something that would help her track down the sick mind that had cut down such a young, vibrant woman in her prime.

"Is it always this bad?" Will asked.

"Sometimes," answered Valerie. "But we can't focus on the violence of it all, Will. If we did, we'd lose our minds. We just have to focus on stopping the killer from doing it again."

"Do you know much about the first murder?" Will said, adjusting his glasses on the bridge of his nose.

"A woman named Cassandra Miller. She was killed in Patapsco Valley State Park. Similar to this, local law enforcement initially thought she had been killed by an animal, until the autopsy revealed it was murder."

"The forensic team is already hiking here," Charlie said as he approached.

"Good," came Valerie's reply.

"Should we go and meet them en route instead of staying... here?" Will asked, clearly unnerved by being so close to such a brutal death scene.

"No," Valerie said solemnly. "There are animals in these woods. And I won't let them touch her. Once the forensic team is here, we'll head out and see what Jackson has to say about the other murder."

CHAPTER SIX

The isolated parking lot made Valerie feel uneasy. It was surrounded by a thick line of pine trees. With the forest so close around her, she couldn't help but think about the victim and how the last thing *she* had seen was the same dark green of the woods.

This remote and empty muddy space for campers and hikers would have been even more ominous if she had not been accompanied by Charlie and Will. Still, Valerie felt a deep desire to be out from underneath the suffocating wilderness and to somewhere more civilized, if such a place existed.

The parking lot was the first place she had encountered on the way back from the crime scene with a strong enough cell signal. Numerous missed calls from her boss, Jackson Weller, meant they had to touch base with him as soon as possible.

Valerie stood with a tablet in her hands with Charlie and Will alongside her at the hood of the car.

"Can you hear us, Chief?" she asked, staring at the webcam feed on the tablet. She hated remote meetings. As a profiler, in-person was always the best way to work, to read people, even colleagues, but since driving back from the national forest to Quantico would take well over two hours, this was the next best thing.

"Yes," Jackson said, his early fifties made more apparent by the poor lighting in his office. "So, where are we with the case?"

"Definite homicide," Valerie said. "A brutal attack, no ID on the victim yet. Jackson, is there a reason you think this kill is connected to the previous one?"

"More of a hunch than anything," Jackson said with a sigh. "I was hoping you'd be able to confirm that. The previous homicide took place four days ago in Patapsco Valley State Park. The report I read said she had been mauled badly after being murdered. Perhaps by a wild animal. It seemed very similar to the case you took a look at today."

"Two killings in parks," Will mused. "It's possible both victims were killed by the same person, but we'd need more to go on to connect them."

"If I can make a suggestion," Charlie added, "perhaps we should stay in the area until tomorrow? The body will have been looked at by the local pathologist by that point. If we have definite info about how the woman here was killed, we might be able to match it to something in the other case."

"That's a good idea, Charlie," Valerie said. "Jackson, could we stay out here for the rest of the evening and do some snooping?"

"Well," Jackson said, his demeanor uncertain, "there's no guarantee the pathologist report will be in first thing tomorrow. It could be another twenty-four hours, maybe longer, you know how these small-time outfits operate. I think it would be best for you to come back to Quantico and look over both cases from here."

A breeze whispered its way through the pine trees, and as the skies darkened, Valerie felt as though the woods themselves were listening in.

There's more here, she thought. Valerie couldn't help but feel they were abandoning the dead girl a little too quickly.

"I understand that, Jackson," Valerie said. "But look, we have one witness. His name is Fred Maxwell. He actually saw the guy who did this—well, his silhouette at least. Given that we know the killer was here a matter of hours ago, and the fact that, going by the terrain, the killer must have knowledge of these woods to have chosen such a secluded spot, there's a very good chance he is still in the area. We could get lucky right off the bat if we just give it one more day."

"I don't know," Jackson said with a distracted look on his face. "I was holding off on telling you all, but we have a meeting with some higher-ups tomorrow morning."

"Why do I not like the sound of that?" said Charlie.

"It's nothing to be alarmed about." Jackson sounded upbeat, but something was off. "It's just that we ruffled a few feathers by getting access to the Clawstitch Killer case files a few weeks ago," he continued. "It seems some higher-ups want to know why we're interested in it. Seemingly someone thinks it's either a waste of our time or a bad allocation of resources."

Valerie felt a pang of guilt.

Jackson and the others had moved mountains to get access to the Clawstitch Killer case, and it was simply so Valerie could right a wrong. That case had always haunted her. Years previous, she had been part of the team investigating the Clawstitch murders, but then she made a mistake that meant he got away. It nearly ended her career, and while the killer had gone cold as far as they knew, she considered the fact that he was still out there somewhere a personal failure.

She had wanted to take another look at the files, and Jackson had made this possible after her success on the Harlow case. But this apparently hadn't gone down well with someone upstairs at the FBI.

"I wonder why they have such a problem with us opening a database on that case?" Will turned to Valerie and gave her a knowing look.

She had explained to him weeks earlier that she had always suspected that the Clawstitch Killer was someone with law enforcement experience.

"And that would be a great reason for you to stay at Quantico and handle the management, Boss," Valerie said. "You know I'd only ruffle more feathers if I was there, and besides, this isn't the Clawstitch Killer case. The trail isn't cold on this one. It's an active killer and there's good reason to believe he's not far from us now. We shouldn't let a few uncomfortable questions from top brass stop us trying to make sure we get *this one* locked up as soon as possible."

There was a brief silence on Jackson's end before he sighed and said, "Alright, but make it quick. I'll give you until two p.m. tomorrow. If you don't have what you need by then, I want you to come back to HQ ASAP. Agreed?"

"Thank you," Valerie said, relieved. "We'll get right on it."

"Stay safe," Jackson said, "and call me when you have anything. No matter how insignificant."

The webcam feed switched off.

"Is he gone?" Will asked.

"Yeah," answered Charlie.

"That's odd that they should be concerned we're looking at the Clawstitch Killer case," pondered Will.

"It could be because the case has gone cold," Charlie pointed out. "But it does seem a bit extreme for them to start evaluating our unit so quickly."

"I just hope they don't revoke access to the files," Valerie said. "I know it's a long shot that we'd ever catch him. But I want to at least have the option."

The sky was darkening quickly. The evening would soon give in to night, and the trees swayed around them as if welcoming the oncoming black skies.

"I don't know if it's because of what we saw up there," observed

Charlie, "but this place gives me the creeps."

"I'm sure it's no more dangerous than any other remote place," said Will. "Might I suggest we find a hotel to stay in for the evening? Perhaps a drink to ease our minds?"

"Okay," Valerie said, walking around to the driver's side of the car. "But just one. I want us to be fresh in the morning. We need to talk to the pathologist and see what he makes of this all. Hopefully we can get an ID on the victim by then, too. As long as we don't know her identify, we're treading water in the dark."

The three investigators got into the car and drove out of the parking lot. As they hit a winding country road, Valerie put her headlights on while Charlie tried to find the nearest hotel.

Will tried to lighten the mood with an embarrassing story about a friend who had once fallen in a river while camping in a similar place. Valerie and Charlie laughed. But a pall fell over the car soon after.

Valerie could feel it in the air.

They were all thinking about the woman's desecrated body in the woods. It was one of the most violent homicides Valerie had ever seen, and she hoped that the man responsible could be caught before another innocent life was butchered so mercilessly.

By the time they arrived at a small, dingy, motel, none of them were in the mood for a drink anymore. They needed sleep, and the hope that the world would be a brighter place the next day.

Valerie knew in her bones that this would not be the case.

CHAPTER SEVEN

Three things had contributed to Valerie's searing headache. The first was the lumpy mattress and pillow she'd wrestled with all night at the motel. The second was the terrible coffee Charlie had discovered at a small bistro on their way into Roanoke City. The final straw was being made to wait in the hall under a buzzing fluorescent light at Roanoke's county coroner's office.

The light flickered almost imperceptibly above Valerie, Will, and Charlie. The corridor was narrow, white, and uninviting. Opposite, the name *Doctor M. Bradlow* hung on a small brown wooden door.

Valerie rubbed her temples and sighed. She looked at her watch: 11 a.m. stared back at her. They only had until 2 p.m. until Jackson wanted them on the road back to Quantico.

"I'm starting to think Dr. Bradlow is avoiding us," she said, sighing.

But Charlie and Will didn't have time to answer. The door opened and out stepped a very small man, no more than five feet tall, with graying hair around the sides and back of his otherwise bald head. On the end of his nose was a pair of gold-rimmed half spectacles.

Valerie thought he looked like someone out of a Dickens novel. But the white lab coat broke that illusion.

"I'm.. I'm terribly sorry," the man said, flustered. "I'm not used to dealing with this sort of thing."

Valerie stood up and shook the man's hand.

"I'm Agent Valerie Law, this is Agent Carlson, and this is Doctor Will Cooper."

"Ah, a doctor, I'm so pleased," the man said. "Perhaps you can assist."

"Well," Will said, "I'm afraid I'm not really that type of a doctor. Are you the local coroner?"

"Yes, yes," the man said, disappointed. "I'm Doctor Bradlow. I've never dealt with…" His face suddenly turned white and he pulled a tissue out from his pocket to pat his sweating brow.

Charlie reached out and held the man's shoulders, stopping him from losing his balance.

"You okay, Doc?" Charlie asked.

"I just… I've been in there for hours. Never… Never seen anything like it."

"Here," Valerie said, helping the man, "have a seat."

Will moved down the hall and retrieved a paper cup of water from a dispenser before handing it to Doctor Bradlow. The doctor's hand shook as he drank it.

"Thank you."

Valerie really felt for the man. She knew that he'd been carrying out the autopsy on the young woman's body. But even Valerie hadn't seen a body so badly torn up like that before. It was particularly bad if it made an experienced doctor question things.

"Never dealt with a homicide before, Dr Bradlow?" Valerie asked.

The doctor looked up, sipping his water.

"Yes, a few times over the years, but usually blunt… blunt force trauma, strangulation, that sort of thing. Never… never this…"

"I know," Valerie said, softly. "It's a lot to take in."

"We don't get a lot of violent deaths around here, you see," the doctor said. "And when we do, most of the time it's an accident. What sort of a man does something like that to a poor young woman?"

"That's what we're here to find out," Charlie said. "With your help, Doctor Bradlow."

"Why don't we move this into your office, Doctor?" suggested Valerie.

The doctor nodded and they walked through the door with Bradlow's name on it. Inside, the office smelled of pipe tobacco. The walls had several pictures of the doctor fishing. And then there were the obligatory medical degrees framed above a small desk.

As the doctor sat down at his desk, Valerie looked at a closed door on the righthand side door.

"That's not…"

The doctor nodded. "Yes, the morgue is in there. We're a small operation."

"I know it's been a difficult autopsy, Doctor Bradlow," offered Charlie. "But don't you think it would be better if you showed us what you found? At the body, I mean."

"If it's all the same to you," the doctor said, as color drained from his face again, "I can give you all of the details here without having to go back in there for now?"

Valerie felt sorry for the man, but given his reluctance to look at the body, she wondered if he was in the right line of work. Seeing gruesome things was an occupational hazard. Though admittedly, this was about as gruesome as things could get.

"Did you take a look at the metal fragments I saw on the bone?" Valerie asked.

"Yes," Doctor Bradlow replied. "I found several more, some on the fibula, collar bone, and the left forearm. I think the latter may have been a defensive wound as she put her hands up to defend herself."

"So, she was conscious when she murdered?" Will asked.

"Technically, she was conscious when she was attacked," continued Doctor Bradlow. "I can't be certain she was aware of everything at the moment of expiration."

Valerie had so many questions running through her head, but she had to stay focused on procedure.

"Do you know which wound proved fatal?"

The doctor shook his head. "Again, I can't be certain, but the left ventricle of the heart was severed during the attack, and that would have certainly done it. Given how the killer... butchered the girl's body, I would suggest some medical knowledge given some of the severed arteries. You could be looking for anyone from a first-year medical student to someone with experience slaughtering... animals."

The doctor patted his forehead with his white handkerchief.

"Do we have any ID on the woman?" Charlie asked.

"No," answered Dr. Bradlow. "Her fingerprints weren't on any national database. But I can say that she's between twenty-three and thirty years old, has previously had her appendix and tonsils removed, and she has an unusual burn on the inside of her left leg."

"From the attack?" Valerie thought back to the location in the woods and was certain there was no evidence of fire.

"No," the doctor said. "I think this was a few years old, at least."

"Can you send me an image of the burn?" Valerie asked.

"Of course."

"And what about the weapon?" Will interjected.

Valerie had a feeling Will was starting to get the hang of field investigations. He knew the right questions to ask.

"That's interesting," the doctor replied. "I haven't had forensics test the metal fragments found in the woman's bones, but I am almost certain there were at least three weapons used."

"Not just one?" Valerie asked. "That's odd."

"Why do you say that?" asked Dr. Bradlow.

"Killers usually dispatch their victims in a moment of frenzy," Valerie explained. "They don't normally have time to switch to different weapons."

"And killers often have a weapon of choice anyway," added Charlie.

"Of course," said Will. "I've interviewed several serial killers who not only had a favorite type of weapon, but a specific weapon they had attachment to. Like a knife that belonged to a family member."

"When I was on my tour," Charlie explained, "guys would sometimes name their rifles."

"Why would they do that?" Dr. Bradlow asked, apparently happy to talk about anything other than the victim's body.

"In war, you rely on your weapon above all else, Doctor Bradlow," Charlie said. "When your life depends on your rifle, you grow attached to it. It can be your best friend. It's hard to explain if you haven't seen combat."

"That's fascinating," Dr. Bradlow said, leaning back in his chair slightly and appearing a little more relaxed.

Valerie was thinking about the different weapons. The reasoning behind them would be important to the profile she was building of the killer.

"Would you say," she asked, "that the three different weapons were used to kill or dismember?"

"One was a knife with a serrated edge, I found markings on the bones. The other two had smoother edges; one was like a small hatchet, maybe."

"And the other?" Valerie said, jotting down some notes into her notepad.

"The other was curious," Dr. Bradlow answered.

"How so?"

"Going by the punctures to the skin and into the muscle tissue, I would say it was curved."

"Like a hook?" Valerie was now more certain than ever that the killer was not a typical serial killer.

"Yes, exactly like a hook."

Charlie let out a nervous laugh. "Wait a minute, I've heard all the old urban legends about killers with hooked hands. I never thought I'd actually have to chase one down."

"Oh, it's too big to be a prosthetic," the doctor explained. "It's more like a small scythe."

Valerie's immediate image was of death. The great harvester carrying his scythe and cutting people down. She'd read about depictions of death throughout the ages for a history class many years previous.

She knew implicitly that the carrying of three weapons was there for a reason. But what that reason was remained obscured.

"When I was talking to a witness," Charlie said, reading from his pocket notepad, "he said he thought the killer was cutting away at the body."

"Oh, yes," the doctor said, taking his glasses off his face and rubbing his eyes. "There's no way you could butcher a body the way he did and have the person still alive through all of it. There's no doubt in my mind that the killer kept cutting well after the poor woman had expired."

A knock sounded at the office door. The doctor jumped, startled.

"Come... Come in..." he said, clearing his throat.

A small woman in her sixties with gray hair in a bob poked her head around the door.

"Ah, Mildred. Everything okay?"

"Yes, Doctor," Mildred said. "There's a Ranger Phillips on the phone, he said to let you know that there are no missing persons cases in Roanoke at the moment."

"Thank you, Mildred."

The lady exited, closing the door behind her.

Valerie heard her feet shuffling away down the hallway outside the room.

"Can you send your full report over to the Criminal Psychopathy Unit in Quantico?" asked Valerie.

"Yes, of course, in a few days I'll..."

"Doctor," Valerie said, sternness settling into her voice, "we don't have a few days. I hate to rush you, but we really need that report. It might help us catch this man before you end up with another nameless victim in your morgue."

Doctor Bradlow looked at the door to the morgue and then back at Valerie.

"Yes, I understand. You'll have it before six p.m. today."

"Thank you, Doctor," Valerie said. She then turned to Charlie. "It sounds like Ranger Phillips has searched the local area for missing persons reports."

"Yeah," Charlie agreed.

"Perhaps the woman was visiting the area?" asked Will. "Could she be from further afield?"

"Most likely," said Valerie. "And remember the worn trail shoe we found. I'd hazard a guess she came here to tackle that Crying Wolf trail, especially if it's notoriously difficult."

"Like a rite of passage," Charlie added. "Some of these hikers are insanely fit. They're always looking for another challenge."

Valerie thought for a moment about how best to identify the victim. "Contact HQ, Charlie, and ask them to run a missing persons search and include the burn mark on the left leg as a possible identifier. Also get someone to do a search online to see if anyone has been chatting about the Crying Wolf trail at George Washington and Jefferson National Forests. We might get lucky and the victim was writing about it online before she came here."

"I hope we find out who she is," Will mused. "If we don't, we don't have much to go on with building a profile. And that could mean…"

"That we won't catch this guy before he kills again," Valerie said, finishing Will's thought for him.

She looked again at the door to the morgue, knowing the woman's desecrated remains lay on the other side, and two jarring thoughts seeped through her mind. *Who are you? And where is your killer?*

CHAPTER EIGHT

I must kill again, the man wrote in his journal. He was hunched over it, and while it was midday outside, the closed blinds of his apartment cast a dim pall on his surroundings.

They will know me! He underlined this over and over.

They had to know him, otherwise it would be for nothing. He wasn't frightened of the police. He wasn't even frightened of the FBI or going to prison for the rest of his life.

No, the only thing that frightened this man was to be forgotten.

For too long he'd watched the world pass by, the unworthy being given adulation while he remained on the sidelines. All his life the man had felt that he was destined for greatness, destined to eclipse all those around him.

But it had never happened.

He blamed bad luck.

Yes, the famous, the lauded, they only had good luck. Why should they have all the attention when he was far more deserving?

Well, he would make the world understand. He would bend it to his will. And with his hands around its throat, he would make it say his name.

Ted Bundy, Jeffrey Dahmer, they were good to study. He read about them in that little apartment. He pored over the newspaper articles and badly written biographies. But this man, *this man*, he would be remembered more than the rest.

But to do that, he would have to kill again. Two victims wasn't enough. He had to have more. And they had to die in more visceral and appalling ways. They had to suffer, and when the public learned of their fate, it would suffer, too.

And the man would rejoice in their suffering and take a bow.

He closed the journal and then slid it into the drawer of his writing desk.

Moving through the dim apartment, he entered his kitchen and poured a glass of milk. He guzzled it down, wiping the rest from his mouth.

Knock, knock.

Someone was there at the door to his apartment.

They can't have caught me yet! he thought as he slammed the empty glass onto the worktop, almost shattering it.

He had only killed his second victim the day before, and he was certain that he had left things as cleanly as possible.

Knock, knock.

There's no way that old man could ID me, he thought to himself as he moved to the apartment door.

In a small closet next to that door, he pulled out a large knife. This was not the knife that he had used the previous day, those weapons of choice were hidden well in another location. But he kept this knife for if the cops came for him.

If he could just get one of them in the neck with the knife, that would add to the infamy he sought.

Keeping the knife behind his back and in a strong grip, he opened the door slowly, just enough to have his face around the side of it. He half expected to be flattened by a wall of law enforcement at that moment.

But instead, an old woman stood before him.

It was Mrs. Goldstein from next hall.

"Hi, Mrs. Goldstein," the man said, smiling. Behind the door, his grip closed on the hilt of the knife.

"I was just wondering," the old lady said from behind a set of equally ancient black-rimmed glasses, "if you could help me. My door has stuck again."

Old bat, he thought. For a moment, the urge came. He wanted to grab the old woman by the hair, drag her inside, and put the knife in her throat.

Calm down, he thought to himself. *Not yet.*

He'd studied the other famous killers. He knew about escalation, about how the desire to kill grows into a frenzy until the killer loses all sense of self-preservation.

That would come. Perhaps. But not right now. If he was to be remembered. He had to choose his victims wisely. Stack them up one by one until the world was forced to remember his name forever.

"Is it stuck, Mrs. Goldstein, what a shame," he said, dropping the knife to the ground. "Of course, I'd be happy to help."

He stepped out of his apartment and walked with the old lady toward her apartment door. He put his hand around her shoulder affectionately. As the old woman prattled on about the landlord needing to fix the lock, that it always stuck no matter what she tried, the man looked at the woman's wrinkled neck.

I could just wrap my fingers around that saggy flesh and twist.

"Let me give it a good throttle," he said loudly to the old woman as he reached the door.

The key was already in the lock, and so he turned it as hard as he could, pulling and pushing on the door handle until there was a loud click.

He felt the lock give way.

He wished that click had been a bone in the old woman's neck.

"Oh, thank you!" The old lady beamed.

"No problem, Mrs. Goldstein," he said, grinning like a Cheshire cat. "Any time I can help, just knock."

Two letters crumpled on the floor as the door moved. She bent down to pick them up.

The man walked back to his apartment with two things on his mind. The first was that he would kill the old woman only when he was certain he was going to get caught. Dispatching an elderly neighbor in a suitably grotesque way would be good for headlines.

The second thought the old lady had unwittingly given to him by picking up the two letters.

Letters, he thought. *The Zodiac did it, so did the Son of Sam, why not me?*

The man would get his words into the press. That would stir things up. That would get them talking.

He closed the door to his apartment and saw the knife lying on the floor. He picked it up. It felt good in his hands.

"You'll do for Mrs. Goldstein," he said to the knife as he put it back in the closet, before grabbing a pen to write something to give him good word of mouth.

My public will love this.

CHAPTER NINE

Valerie stood outside the diminutive police station in Roanoke. The stark beauty of the Blue Mountains behind was a welcome reprieve to her. She looked off toward them, thinking of the cool air. How nice it would be to be standing at their summit and looking down at the world, far removed from the horrors of what had happened to the woman in the woods.

At least something positive had happened in the last few hours. A family had reported that a woman about the same age as the victim had gone missing. They had driven down to Roanoke as soon as law enforcement spoke with them.

"Well, he isn't happy," Charlie said, walking across the parking lot.

"Oh, dear," Will said, standing next to Valerie. "I can't say I've seen him angry before, but then I haven't known him as long as you both."

"Did you tell Jackson that we think we've ID'd the body?" Valerie asked.

"Yup," said Charlie, putting his cell phone into his pocket. "That's about the only thing that bought us more time. I think he's just on edge. That meeting with the higher-ups about the Clawstitch Killer case didn't go well."

"What did he say happened?" asked Will.

"Not much," Charlie replied. "But he sounded like a disgruntled bear on the phone, so I'm guessing it was a bit of a train wreck."

Valerie sighed inwardly. She'd promised Jackson they'd be on the road by 2 p.m., but now it was 4 o'clock. The last couple of hours had been a rabbit hole she was required to explore.

"It was essential that we know who the victim was before leaving, higher-ups be damned."

"Ranger Phillips says the family is inside," Charlie said in a somber voice.

"This is the part of the job I hate the most," Valerie said as the three friends began walking over to the police station.

"I'm not sure what to expect," Will said.

"Will," offered Charlie, "it's never easy talking to the victim's family, but if you can maintain some distance, we could find out something important."

"Let's start with making sure it is the victim's family," Valerie said, opening the door into the police station.

Inside, a young officer in his twenties sat behind the front desk. He looked bored to Valerie. His eyes lit up at the presence of visitors.

"Hello, how can I help you?" he said, cheerily.

Valerie showed her ID. "I'm Agent Law with the Criminal Psychopathy Unit in Quantico. We're here to talk with the Bridges family."

"Oh, right, of course. Right this way," the officer said, leading them through another doorway.

As they walked down a corridor, the officer seemed to be filling in the silence nervously.

"Terrible thing," he said. "I'm just glad she wasn't from around here."

"I don't think it matters where she was from," Valerie said pointedly before softening. "But I understand why you wouldn't want such a thing to happen to one of your own."

"So, do you deal with sort of thing often?" the young police officer asked, sounding a little nervous.

"All the time," Charlie answered.

"Must be hard."

"It is," Valerie replied.

They turned a corner and Valerie was happy to see a familiar face standing by a closed interview door.

Ranger Phillips.

"Hi," Valerie said.

"Hello, Agent Law," Phillips replied. "We have a mother and a sister in this room. We can't be sure they are the family, but they came down as soon as you contacted them."

"Thank you, Ranger Phillips."

Valerie opened the door.

Inside, a woman in her fifties with black hair was sitting, her hands clenched on her lap. Alongside her, a younger woman, Valerie estimated in her early twenties, was comforting the older woman.

"Hello," Valerie said. She could feel her heart racing. She truly hated this part of the job. "I'm Agent Law, I believe Agent Carlson spoke on the phone with you a few hours ago?"

"Yes," the older woman said. "I'm Diane Bridges, and this is my daughter Melanie."

"It's nice to meet…"

"Is it her?" the daughter said sharply, tears in her eyes.

"That's what we're going to find out," Valerie answered. She took off her coat and sat across a small table from them.

Will and Charlie sat either side of her.

"Agent Carlson was able to find mention on the website Wild Trekking that your older daughter, Shelly, was going to head to George Washington and Jefferson National Forests yesterday. Would that be correct?"

"Yes," Mrs. Bridges said. "She was always trekking around the country. I told her she needed to be more careful always going alone, but she—" The woman began to sob.

"My sister," Melanie added, "loved adventure. She was always pushing herself to trek more difficult trails."

Valerie winced inside when she heard Melanie refer to her sister in the past tense. It was a sure sign she already suspected the victim was Shelly Bridges.

"The moderator on Wild Trekking was instrumental in helping us contact you, Mrs. Bridges," said Charlie. "He told us Shelly was training for a trip on the Appalachian Trail later in the year?"

"Yes, that's right," answered Mrs. Bridges. "It was on her bucket list, as she used to call it."

The idea of a woman in her mid-twenties needing a bucket list of things to do before she died saddened Valerie. How many entries on that list would now go unanswered?

Valerie pulled out her cell phone and skipped to an image.

"Mrs. Bridges," she said, softly, "did Shelly have a burn mark on the inside of her leg?"

Mrs. Bridges began sobbing again. She couldn't get the words out.

"Yes," answered Melanie. "When we were teenagers, she had an accident while climbing on some pipes outside a local factory. One of the other kids bet her she couldn't climb up the side of the building. She took that bet, but she didn't realize there was steam running through one of the pipes. She stretched her leg out while up there to grab onto one and got a terrible burn on her skin."

"I'm very sorry, but given everything you've told us," Valerie said, "it's very likely that the body we found is Shelly's."

Mrs. Bridges let out a cry of pain and Melanie tried her best to comfort her. They both cried into each other's arms, and a little piece of Valerie broke down at the sight. She thought about her own mother and sister. They were in pain too, though of a different kind.

"I'm so sorry," Will now said, speaking for the first time. "There's nothing we can say to take away your pain, but we will do everything we can to bring the man responsible to justice."

"So..." Melanie struggled through the words. "So, she was murdered?"

"Yes, I'm afraid so," answered Will.

"How?" asked Mrs. Bridges, rubbing her eyes. "How did the bastard do it?!"

"The autopsy shows that she was stabbed a number of times," Valerie said, trying her best to be as straight as possible. "You'll probably end up reading about it in the press, so you have to prepare yourself for the details. Melanie was brutally murdered, and the killer attacked her body even after the point of death."

The resulting cries from mother and daughter were unbearable. But Valerie and her team had to bear them. They had to for their own sanity.

"Can I get you anything?" Charlie said, his voice gentle. "A coffee or some water?"

They both shook their heads.

"Mrs. Bridges," Charlie continued, "I can't imagine how difficult this is for you, but the hours and days after a homicide are the most critical. We need you to answer just a few more questions to help us catch your daughter's murderer."

"I think she's done enough for today!" Melanie said, sharply.

"No," Mrs. Bridges said through tears. "I want to, Melanie. For your sister's sake."

For a moment, Valerie panicked. She didn't see Mrs. Bridges and Melanie across from her. For a moment, she saw her own mother sobbing and her sister, Suzie, by her side, in a way Valerie never had been with their mother. Her heart raced.

Is this the illness coming? Valerie thought. *Do I start seeing things? Do I fall to pieces?*

She snapped herself out of it with one thought: *The killer is out there. That's all that matters.*

"Mrs. Bridges," said Valerie, "it's very unlikely that the killer randomly came across your daughter on the trail. The Crying Wolf trail is overgrown and seldom used. In fact, it's only known by those with a keen interest in hiking. The killer came equipped to kill. But he had no way to know that someone would be on that trail the other night. It's likely he somehow knew where your daughter would be."

"You mean… someone Shelly knew killed her?" Melanie said in disbelief.

"No, it doesn't quite mean that," said Valerie. "But it's a possibility. It's also possible it was a stranger whom she dealt with online. It could have been another member of the Wild Trekking forum where she posted her plans."

"There's just one problem with that, though," Charlie interjected. "She said publicly in a forum post that she was going to the Crying Wolf trail, but she never said when."

"For that reason," continued Valerie, "we need to account for anyone who would have known *when* she was planning this trip. Can you help us with that?"

"Yes," answered Mrs. Bridges. "We knew she was coming here yesterday. But she didn't post anything on Facebook about the specific day. She didn't like to do that because she was always worried someone would use that to break into her apartment while she was out of town."

Valerie thought for a moment.

"So, you think," she asked, "that it's unlikely Shelly would have posted anywhere on social media about the exact day she was coming?"

"Well," Melanie replied, "she wouldn't have stated the day. She might have mentioned it somewhere, but I didn't see it, and I don't know who she would have told other than us, in person or over a call."

"No friends she would have confided in?" Valerie was beginning to feel frustrated by any leads.

"Maybe," said Melanie. "But she was very independent. We didn't really know a lot about her private life because she kept that to herself."

"Yes," said Mrs. Bridges. "Except for one night a week when we'd have a family meal. That was non-negotiable. We'd see each other then, and at special occasions. She… She loved to tell us about her adventures more than her relationships."

"Any boyfriends or girlfriends?" Charlie asked.

Mrs. Bridges began to cry again. "She wanted kids. But later on. She wanted to make the most of her twenties first."

"Could you excuse us for a moment?" Valerie said.

The three investigators left the room together and quietly spoke in the corridor.

"Thoughts?" Valerie asked.

Charlie frowned for a moment. "We're going to need a complete rundown of Shelly's social media profiles, see if she maybe let something slip about being here yesterday. Though it looks unlikely."

"Perhaps, if I may," said Will, "we shouldn't be so quick to dismiss the idea that the killer was prowling the woods."

"Why do you say that?" asked Valerie.

"Several years ago, I was working on a theory about missing persons cases in America's national forests," Will explained. "There are many strange disappearances, and while conspiracy theorists like to invoke aliens and Bigfoot as explanations, I came to the conclusion that it's possible there are serial killers who camp in remote locations and look for opportunities."

"It's possible," said Valerie. "But I think it's much more likely that the killer came here deliberately for Shelly. We'll work with both hypotheses for now. Charlie, you get the social media info you can from the Bridges, and find out more about her work life. There's got to be something in her personal relationships."

"What are you going to do?" asked Charlie.

"I'm going to phone Jackson again, tell him we won't be back at Quantico for another few hours. I'm sure that'll go down well. Will, could you sit in with Charlie and see if there's any more insight?"

"Yes, of course."

Charlie had a puzzled look on his face. Valerie knew what that was. It was unusual for her to step out of an interview like that. But she had to leave. She moved out of the building and breathed in the cool air.

The image of Melanie defending her mother had brought it all home again. Suzie had defended their mother, too, despite what she had done to them as kids.

But not Valerie. She couldn't forgive.

The cold air washed over Valerie's face. She could feel her own emotions seeping into the case, and that could only lead to dark places.

Valerie dialed Jackson's number.

"Oh, thank you so much for calling, Agent Law," he said sarcastically.

"I'm really sorry, Jackson," Valerie said. "We're with the family. I think we've ID'd the victim."

Jackson sighed. "Well, not a wasted day then?"

"No," Valerie said. "I'm really sorry if us not being there causes issues with the higher-ups."

"It's okay," Jackson said. "I'll just play darts on a photo of you and Charlie for a bit. That will make me feel better."

"That bad?"

"It think we've trampled on some toes asking for access to the Clawstitch Killer case," Jackson said. "But I told them you were our best agent and I'd put my neck on the line if it meant you got a second bite at the apple."

"Thank you, Boss."

"Don't thank me, let's just try and focus on your current case," he said. "What's your next move?"

"We'll not get back to HQ now until after seven p.m. at least."

"No need," said Jackson. "The higher-ups are gone."

"In that case," said Valerie, "I'd like to look into the other killing you mentioned today. The one you think might have been committed by the same man."

"Yes, that would be prudent. Keep me appraised."

"I will," said Valerie. "We'll finish up here and head home."

The call ended.

She looked around her in the parking lot to the city of Roanoke, the mountains in the background frozen in time. It was beautiful. But beauty could be sullied, and it had been there.

"*The woods are lovely, dark and deep,*" she said to herself, quoting the Robert Frost poem again. "*But I have promises to keep, and miles to go before I sleep.*"

Yes, Roanoke was beautiful, and she hoped it would never be stained again by such a barbaric murder.

CHAPTER TEN

Posting the letter was not so simple. The man knew he could not be seen. Worse, he could not leave any trace of his DNA on the letter and envelope. That way, he could never be traced by the police.

He had written it in a classic sense, using cut up letters from newspapers. He carefully wore latex gloves, his hair protected by a shower cap and his breath covered by a surgical mask. That would surely be enough to stop any trace of DNA.

Posting it, he took another precaution.

He did not want anyone to recognize him, so he wore a simple disguise. Old clothes he'd bought from a thrift store were the exact opposite of what he'd normally be seen in. Then, sunglasses and a beanie hat. Finally, brown mustache and goatee stuck to his chin and upper lip using some spirit glue.

No one will know.

He felt a sense of elation as he reached a postbox. No one was paying any attention to him. And why should they? This was not his real self. The person they *would* pay attention to was the killer beneath. The one capable of anything.

I'll haunt their dreams, he thought as he slid the letter into the postbox, letting go of it.

As he walked home, he entered a public park, children playing. For a moment, he watched them. He remembered being a child. He remembered pretending to smile. He wondered if they pretended, too.

It was all pretend for him. A game. A theatrical show.

How he'd pulled the wool over everyone's eyes. Even those who thought they knew him did not. They didn't know how he really felt about the world, about being special yet being unheard.

In a public bathroom, he walked into one of the stalls. It smelled of urine. Someone had peed on the toilet seat and left it like that.

And they'll think I'm *depraved,* he thought. *Just look at how they all behave.*

Taking off his disguise, he changed into other clothes and left the bathroom behind. He left the park and then ditched the bag of clothes in a large garbage container down the back of a small alley.

After that, he went to his favorite coffee house and bought a mocha latte.

He watched through the glass window at the people walking by.

He grinned. Out there he would find other victims. They too would be going about their lives, not knowing that their days were numbered. Not knowing that a wolf was about to pounce and take everything from them.

And when his letter would be published by the newspapers—that's when his infamy would grow. And that's when the public would finally start to understand.

This man was special.

This man was one of a kind.

This man should never have been ignored.

He sipped his mocha and settled, relaxation being something that seldom came to him.

For once he could enjoy it. He looked once more to the world outside.

They have no idea what's coming.

CHAPTER ELEVEN

Standing outside of Charlie's car, Valerie felt a slight pattering of rain on her head to add to the gray concrete all around.

The case was in her veins now. She was hooked.

She knew that if Shelly Bridges was connected to the first victim, then she could start to build a proper profile of the killer. What his motivation was. Who could be his next target. But speaking with the original victim's father was proving difficult.

"I never thought we'd be waiting outside a burger joint to do an interview," she said to Charlie.

"It's our best shot, Val."

"I feel like we're being haunted by a series of worsening parking lots," Will groaned.

And it was true.

This was the third such parking lot in two days. But instead of the beauty of Roanoke, they were now in Baltimore, in an area Valerie would have affectionately referred to as a fixer-upper.

"You don't feel very safe in a place like this, do you?" Will asked, almost rhetorically, glaring at the broken concrete and run-down homes behind the less-than-appealing burger joint.

A neon sign flashed above with the word "Luther's" in bright purple. The "s" had gone out and was yet to be repaired.

"I grew up in a neighborhood like this, Will," Charlie said. "Don't judge a book by its cover. You find good and bad people all over."

"Sorry, Charlie," Will said. "I didn't mean to sound like a snob."

"Ah, don't worry," Charlie replied. "That road goes both ways. I'm sure if I hung out with you and your professor buddies, I might feel a little out of place myself."

"For what it's worth," Will offered, "I think you could run intellectual circles around them."

Charlie smiled and patted Will on the back. "Hey, Val. I think we should keep this one."

"Yeah," replied Valerie. "But we might need to get him chipped in case he runs away."

"Your jokes are mesmerizing," Will said.

Valerie looked at the burger joint.

"Charlie. You go around the back. Will, you come with me."

Will nodded as Charlie moved off around to the side of the building.

Valerie and Will entered the burger joint. It smelled like fries and grease. A counter ran across the narrow room, a waitress standing behind it serving a couple of ominous-looking customers sitting on stools.

"Hey, Mary," one of the customers said. "Where's the relish on this?"

Mary the waitress leaned over the counter, lifted the top bun of the man's burger, then grabbed a relish bottle and squeezed a dollop onto the patty.

She then squeezed the bun back on top.

"I hope you washed yer hands," the man grumbled, taking a bite of his burger.

"Matty, I think you're the last person that should be talkin' to people about their hygiene."

The waitress turned from the regulars and walked to the nearest end of the counter where Valerie and Will were now sitting. Valerie smelled cigarettes and coffee in equal measure, and she was pretty sure they were both coming from Mary.

"Hi." Mary beamed, her weathered face still retaining a kindness when she smiled. "What can I get for ya?"

"I'm looking for an old friend of mine, Luther Miller, is he around?" Valerie asked.

"Looking for? What are ya, Feds or somethin'?" Mary joked.

"This is an old friend of Luther's from Baltimore Pen," Valerie said, pointing to Will.

Will opened his mouth to protest.

"Unfortunately, he lost his voice in an accident a few years ago," Valerie said, cutting Will off. "I'm just here as his chaperone. Could you ask Luther if he's got a few minutes to talk?"

"Sure," Mary said, eyeing Valerie and Will suspiciously. Mary walked through the door at the back of the counter.

"Hey, Luther," she shouted loudly. "There's an old jailbird pal of yours here to see ya."

"What? Who!?" a grizzled voice from the kitchen replied.

Footsteps soon joined the voice, and a disheveled man in a white apron appeared through the doorway looking around with a smile on his face.

"Where is he?" the man asked. He seemed hopeful that he would spy a familiar face, but quickly his eyes trained onto Valerie and Will at the end of the counter.

Mary came back into the room and pointed at the two investigators.

"That's the guy there," she said.

"I don't know him." The man stared.

Valerie stood up. "I'm sorry for the ruse, Mr. Miller, but I had to make certain that you were here. I know you refused to speak to us earlier when we called."

The man suddenly darted for the door into the back, and then a commotion could be heard outside around to the rear of the building.

"Why is he running?" asked Will.

"Come on, Will," Valerie said, rushing out of the building and around to the back alley.

When she and Will appeared around the corner outside, Charlie was in the process of detaining Luther Miller.

"I didn't do nothing," the man protested.

Charlie had a firm hold of him. "We're not here to arrest you. We just want to know about your daughter."

"Man, I told you on the phone. She's not my daughter, she's my stepdaughter."

"And you don't seem too concerned about what's just happened to her, Mr. Miller," Valerie observed. "Or should I say, Mr. Tarrant."

The man looked up at Valerie. "Yeah, yeah, okay, you found me."

"I'm a bit confused," said Will.

"You're not the only one, buddy," the man sneered.

"Mr. Tarrant," Valerie said, "I'm not interested in your string of fake names. Speaking with some colleagues at Quantico, I'm quite aware that you are, or at least have been in the past, an FBI informant. I also understand that you may be frightened of speaking so publicly with agents given your colorful past with organized crime. But be all that as it may. I'm only interested in finding the person who brutally murdered your stepdaughter a few days ago. And I would think you would want the same thing."

"You help us with this," Charlie said, "and we'll be on our way."

The smell of rotting garbage was swirling around the alley, and Valerie hoped they wouldn't have to stay there for too long.

"Okay, okay," Mr. Tarrant said. "What do you want to know?"

Charlie loosened his grip and let the man stand on his own.

"You don't seem overly concerned with the fact that your stepdaughter is dead, Mr. Tarrant?" Will said, half question, half observation.

"She was dead to me a long time ago," he said. "I'm sad about what happened to her. But I was only around for a few years. She ended up being more trouble than she was worth after her mother died. It's not like I raised her for long."

Valerie felt like slapping the man across the face and giving him a good shake. The fact that he could so easily turn his back on someone who was once under his care spoke volumes.

But Valerie had to put these feelings to the side.

"When did you last speak with your stepdaughter?"

"I don't know, a few weeks ago, I think," the man said, scratching his head. "She came around here looking for some money. I gave her some then told her I didn't want to see her again. But I knew she'd come back. She always does... did."

"And why did you want to disconnect from her, Mr. Tarrant?" Will asked.

Valerie was happy to see that Will was slowly taking on the investigator mantle.

"Cassandra, she was a good kid when she was younger," Mr. Tarrant said. For the first time he showed some emotion. Valerie could sense a slight shaking of his voice.

"I did love her," he said. "But she started hanging around with the wrong crowd, and then a couple years ago she gets a DUI, runs some guy over. She just went off the rails after that."

"And you just abandoned her?" Charlie said.

Valerie implicitly knew that Charlie was thinking of his own kids. The idea of abandonment was so alien to him. And on more than one occasion on cases, he had dropped his professional guard to show his displeasure at what he called "runaway dads."

This time was no different.

"Yeah, maybe," the man said. "Cassandra was sued for thousands of dollars after that DUI. I paid it out of my own pocket. My life savings gone. Maybe I would have mellowed over time, but whenever she came 'round here with her hand out looking for more, I just learned to hate what she'd become. I know she recently said she was getting her act together. But I didn't believe her."

"Do you know of anyone who would have wanted to harm

Cassandra?" Valerie asked, taking her notebook out ready to jot down names.

The man laughed before catching himself in an all too jovial moment.

"I don't know who she was running with lately. But she had borrowed money all over the city. I guess there'd be a lot of people who wouldn't be too happy about that."

"Can you give us some names?" Charlie asked.

Tarrant shook his head. "I don't know any more than that. But when a girl ends up on the streets, it either ends in them getting out or giving up. I think she gave up."

"So you don't know anything about your stepdaughter's death?" Valerie pressed.

"Nothing," Mr. Tarrant answered.

Valerie was sensing another dead end up ahead. The frustration was bubbling underneath. She let out a sigh, audible for all to hear.

"Okay, Mr. Tarrant," Valerie said. "Stick around for a while. We may want to talk to you again. And if you try to run, that's going to make me very suspicious."

The man didn't say anything, he just disappeared back into the burger joint.

The three investigators walked back to their car out front.

"He could be involved," Charlie said. "He does have a rap sheet as long as the Mississippi."

"Are we sure these two victims are even related?" asked Will.

"You're uncertain?" Valerie inquired

"Well, we weren't able to look directly at the crime scene," said Will. "But from the report I read back at the office, the murders of Cassandra and then Shelly at the national forest are markedly different."

"It was Jackson's call," Valerie said. "It was the close proximity in deaths and the fact that both bodies were butchered badly. Though Shelly much worse than Cassandra."

"But that would fit into escalation," added Charlie. "If the killer started off feeling his way into the kill with Cassandra, then became more violent with Shelly. That would make sense."

"Yes, it would," said Valerie mournfully. "But it also means that the next victim's death will be even worse."

"Any ideas about the perp's psychology, yet?" Charlie asked.

"Not yet," Valerie said. "We need more data. Let's keep digging."

"The biggest problem is that the two victims couldn't have been more different," Will observed. "Cassandra's life was a mess, she had been a drunk for much of her short life. Then Shelly was successful. Outgoing. Stable by all accounts."

"We can't even say there's a connection with how they looked," Charlie mused. "Cassandra was dark haired, Shelly fair. Cassandra was just under five feet tall, but Shelly was decently over that. Complexion, eye color, it's almost as if the killer deliberately chose two victims as different from each other as possible, if indeed it is the same killer."

Valerie's ears pricked up at that.

"You know, that's not a bad idea," she said. "What if the killer is deliberately picking different victims so we can't build a profile?"

"That would be clever," said Will. "But can we honestly say a butcher like this man would have the faculties to be so conniving? There was so much violence in Shelly's death, it's difficult to see a killer together enough in his mind to do that and be cognizant of picking varied victims."

"It wouldn't be unheard of," Valerie answered as they reached the car. "But it would be rare."

"It's starting to look like the only connection we have is that both victims were murdered in parks," Will said, his voice sounding dejected. "I'm worried that we'll only be able to build a profile if he kills again, and that's the last thing anyone wants."

"If the only thing connecting the victims," Valerie said, getting into the car, "is that they are women, then every woman within a few hundred miles of here is in danger."

Valerie clipped in her seat belt and rolled down her window.

"Where to now?" Charlie asked. "We'll follow."

"There must be a profile of the killer," Valerie whispered under her breath.

Will rested his hand on the outside of the car roof. "Maybe there isn't one, or too obscure for us to figure out."

"I don't want to believe that," Valerie said. "You two go home, it's going to be a long few days."

"Why do I get the feeling you're not going home, too?" Charlie asked.

Valerie thought about her apartment. But she just couldn't face it. Her mind was telling her there was more to be discovered, she just had to pull at the thread for it to be revealed.

CHAPTER TWELVE

Valerie found the offices eerie in the evening. The low hum of the air conditioning above her head was all she could hear. That and the occasional footsteps from somewhere on the floor, no doubt another agent putting in overtime at the Mesmer Building like she was.

Staring at the evidence board, Valerie was trying to put together the two murder victims. The coffee in her hand was getting cold, and the attempts to build a usable profile for the killer even colder.

Valerie's phone rang, Sheryl Crow's "Run Baby Run" playing as the ring tone.

"Hey, Tom," Valerie said.

"I just thought I'd check in," Tom said. "Do you not think it's time to call it a day?"

Valerie looked to the clock on the wall. It read 9:30 p.m. She was tired. She was ready to quit. But she had to find a connection between the two murders; she felt it was there waiting to be found.

"Just a little bit longer," she said, taking a sip of her lukewarm coffee.

"Okay," Tom said. "Remember, tomorrow's date night, though. I have you all to myself."

"I'll remember, honey. Let's order in pizza."

Tom laughed and sighed almost simultaneously. "I'm not an idiot, you know?"

"That obvious, huh?"

"Val," Tom said, "you may be the profiler, but I'm getting pretty good at reading you myself. You only ever tell me to order in pizza so I don't go to the bother of cooking for us. That way, if you have to cancel because of the case, you won't feel as bad about it."

"I'm sorry, Tom," Valerie said. "I just know there's a connection between these two murder victims. There has to be."

"You know, sometimes I think you lock yourself up in your office at night because you don't want to deal with what's going on in your real life."

It was obvious. It was playschool psychology. But that didn't

56

matter. Valerie knew there was a grain of truth to it. Keeping busy meant she didn't have to think about Suzie or her mom.

"I'm not avoiding things, Tom. I'm just trying to catch this guy before he kills anyone else."

"I wish I could help, but that's well outside of my skill set. Just don't work too hard, Val. And if you can try and be there tomorrow, that would be great. I'd like you all to myself."

"I'll do my best. Good night, Tom."

Valerie stood looking at the evidence board, photographs of the murder victims and where they were found hung hauntingly like a macabre gallery. Suddenly, Valerie's mind was churning around something else.

"I'd like you all to myself." Valerie repeated Tom's words, and they sparked a memory. Something Valerie had seen the previous day but had yet to follow up on.

She rushed around to her desk, sat down, and opened up a browser on her computer. She went straight to Shelly Bridges' Facebook page. She looked through the profile, and there it was. She had only joined Facebook six weeks before her murder.

This was curious to Valerie. After all, Shelly was a keen online user. She had been documenting her training for the Appalachian Trail on the Wild Trekking forums. She also had a number of other social media accounts, all years old, so why then would her Facebook page be so new?

A thought began to permeate in Valerie's consciousness.

Shelly was trying to get away from something.

Valerie did a search of Shelly's name on Facebook, and there it was. An older account. Still active. Valerie knew that leaving an older Facebook page active was a strategy employed by those trying to avoid online stalkers. It would act as a decoy of a kind. Undesirable people could peruse that profile, while the user would use the new profile for family and friends.

Looking through the older profile, Valerie saw that several people had left memorial messages. Most of them were of the common kind. Rest in peace. Can't believe you're gone, etc. Looking through the messages, Valerie saw that a few of Shelly's friends had taken exception to a man named Darryl Minski. He had left a message saying how sad he was to hear about her passing. But some of Shelly's other friends called him a creep, and told them that he had made Shelly feel uncomfortable.

Now Valerie's mind was alight with the possibility that she was looking at the very man who had murdered Shelly.

Valerie knew the first victim, Cassandra, didn't have a Facebook page, but she did have an Instagram page. It took Valerie only a few minutes to find comments on Cassandra's Instagram photos by one Darryl Minski. All talking about Cassandra's "beautiful smile."

Did you want them all to yourself, Darryl? Did you?

She might not have found the personality profile of the killer, but Valerie knew she had stumbled across something better than that.

A prime suspect.

CHAPTER THIRTEEN

The 9mm felt cold in Valerie's hand. The ambient rain and night breeze from outside had chilled everything around it. Now indoors, running through an apartment complex with her partner, the cold still hanging on as best it good.

Charlie nodded and moved along the hallway to number 26. He pointed to the door.

Valerie acknowledged and then rushed across the carpeted floor to the opposite side of the doorway. She could feel the tension in the air. There hadn't been time to involve Will in the pursuit of the suspect, and she was glad. She felt implicitly as though things could get very dangerous, very quickly. While Will was a brilliant profiler, she did still worry for his safety out in the field.

Charlie thumped his fist against the door.

"FBI," Valerie shouted. "Open up!"

The two agents waited for a sign of life. Nothing came.

"Darryl Minski, FBI! Open up or we're coming in!"

Again, there was no response.

Just as Valerie was getting ready to put her shoulder through the door, a sound finally arrived. But it came from down the corridor. One of the other apartment doors had opened.

An elderly lady leaned her head out looking down the corridor.

"What's all the fuss happening out here?" the lady said in a creaking voice.

"We're FBI agents," Charlie said. "Please get back inside."

"I'll do no such thing," the old lady said. She stepped out into the full view of the corridor wearing a white nightdress. "You can't come here making all this racket. Bothering nice Mr. Minski. You leave him alone."

The thought of this man being nice reminded Valerie of what neighbors always said about such people after being caught. *He was a quiet man. Kept to himself.*

They all were like that on the outside, except when they revealed their true, depraved selves.

Valerie knew she'd have to act quick to defuse the situation. If Minski was the type of brutal killer she thought he might be, then he was capable of anything. Valerie had to make sure no innocents were caught in the crossfire.

She rushed along the corridor and holstered her weapon.

"What's your name?" she said quietly. "Mine is Valerie. But you can call me Val."

The old lady seemed caught off guard by Valerie's tact. It was as if she was readying for a good verbal joust, when she was suddenly met with a smiling face and a soft voice. Valerie was always good at deescalating arguments when needed.

She knew sometimes she had to take the soft approach. The trick was knowing when to be approachable and then when to be a little rougher.

"Eh, Gladys, dear," the old lady said. "What's all this that's going on?"

"Well, Gladys," Valerie explained, "we think Mr. Minski might be in danger. We have to get into the apartment to help. And we don't want to go into too much detail, but there may be a danger to others as well. So please, Gladys, for me, could you step back inside? I'd hate to see you get hurt."

The old lady patted Valerie on the cheek. "You're a sweetheart. I wish my daughter was as well-mannered as you. I do hope Mr. Minski is okay, he's been out hiking a lot and coming and going. He seems tired whenever I see him."

Alarm bells were now ringing in Valerie's mind. The man had been hiking... Had two of those hikes been to chase down and brutally murder the two victims?

This was enough for Valerie. She was growing more certain that she had her man. And she was going to either arrest him or get into that apartment to find the evidence she needed.

As the old lady began to talk about her daughter and how she never called her even at Christmas, Valerie was able to usher her back into her apartment.

Valerie readied herself once more, drew her weapon, and joined Charlie by Darryl Minski's door yet again.

"One chance, Darryl," Valerie said, loudly. "It's your last, and then we are coming in."

The seconds passed. It was time to act. Now.

Valerie stepped back and thrust her foot forward, smacking against the door handle. The door rattled but didn't give.

Valerie saw an image in her mind of what the killer had done to Shelly Bridges and Cassandra Miller before that. Anger coursed through her veins. Charlie stepped up to try the door, but Valerie was too quick.

This time she used that anger. She thrust her shoulder against the door.

She practically took it off its hinges.

The lock buckled and they were inside in a flash.

Charlie was at Valerie's back immediately as they entered the darkened hall of Darryl Minski's apartment.

"Slow down," Charlie whispered.

But Valerie was having none of it.

All she could think of was the two butchered women. She'd put a stop to it. There wouldn't be a third.

Valerie moved from one room to the next, sweeping through carefully but with purpose. She was on a mission, but she would not forget her training.

"He's not here," Valerie said.

"Yeah," Charlie answered, disappointed. "Let's take a look around, see if we can find anything."

Valerie switched on a few lights. The apartment looked like any other. Clean and organized. Valerie could smell bleach.

"I wonder if he was cleaning something up or trying to get rid of evidence," she said, hopeful. Valerie continued to look around. In Darryl's bedroom she found a closet. When she opened it, her eyes were drawn to a box on a shelf.

Looking inside, she pulled out a ring binder. Charlie watched as Valerie opened it.

Valerie couldn't believe her eyes. Page after page was filled with women. Photos clearly taken without their knowledge.

She looked on in horror at the faces, women going about their days being stalked and photographed. Then, on one page, she saw several photos of Cassandra Miller.

"My God," she said. "Look." She handed the binder to Charlie.

It wasn't long before Charlie made his own grim discovery. On one of the last pages, there were three photos of Shelly Bridges out hiking. Darryl Minski had taken photographs of her while apparently hiding in the woods.

"Do you think that was just before he killed her?" Charlie asked.

"It's possible," Valerie said, her heart breaking at the sight of a proud, strong young woman out enjoying the outdoors, unaware that she was about to die at the hands of a brutal killer.

"We need to put out an APB for his arrest right away," Valerie said.

But Charlie held up his hands for a moment.

"Do you hear something?" Valerie asked, knowing that her partner's hearing was legendary.

"Someone's coming down the corridor outside... Now they've stopped at the doorway."

Valerie readied herself, her heart beating fast, knowing she was about to come face to face with the killer.

They rushed around the corner and grabbed the figure of a man standing in the broken doorway.

"What the hell is going on?" the man said, struggling as Charlie put cuffs on him.

He then looked past them. Through a doorway, he clearly could see the open closet, the ring binder with the photographs of his victims on the floor.

He then went limp, giving in to the inevitable. He'd been found.

"You got him?" Valerie said, still pointing her gun.

"Yeah, I got him," Charlie said.

Valerie felt the surge of excitement There was nothing like the thrill of catching a killer.

Now it was time for Valerie to get into his head and find out if there were any more victims out there to be identified.

CHAPTER FOURTEEN

Tanya Brenning was getting tired. It had been a long few days for her. She had been in wrangles with some of her suppliers, but thankfully her store was now fully stocked for the next day.

It was 8 p.m., and it was practically night outside. She had stayed longer than she had intended, but Tanya took pride in the displays in her store window.

She had recently been spurred on to even higher standards than before by a community award granted by the local Chamber of Commerce. As she was tidying up, she looked at it hanging on the wall above her counter. It had been a rough few years, but her business was finally making a regular profit. All of her hard work was finally paying dividends.

Tired yet happy, Tanya closed up for the night. She entered in the alarm code, closed the door behind her into the street outside, and then pulled down the metal shutters.

After locking the shutters, Tanya moved off out from the storefront down a side street. Her car was parked beneath the bright light of a streetlamp.

She walked over to the car and started to feel unsettled. It was the type of nervousness that a person feels while being watched. She couldn't shake the feeling, and that nervousness made her search quickly in her handbag for her car keys.

She looked up from her handbag, keys finally in hand, but her heart almost stopped dead at what she saw. In the reflection of the driver's window, a hooded figure stood behind her.

She let out a sharp gasp and turned quickly.

"I'm sorry," the man wearing the black hoodie said. "I didn't mean to frighten you."

He smiled, and Tanya looked to her left and right quickly, glancing to see if there was anyone else around. She had never felt so alone.

"I was just wondering," the man said, "if you wouldn't mind giving me a jump start. There's no one else around here at the moment and my battery has gone dead. I'm parked just in front of you. It'll only take a second."

Tanya felt an immediate need to get away. She'd have run down the street and tried to find someone else out there beneath the night lights, but the man was standing just in front of her, and he would have easily grabbed her the second she tried to move.

"I'd rather not, if you don't mind." Tanya glared at the man.

The man's grin quickly faded. For a moment he said nothing. Tanya could hear the highway nearby; the passing cars had never felt so distant.

"I'm only asking for your help," the man said, his voice stern. "I just need a jump start. Otherwise I'll have to call a towing service, that's gonna cost me an arm and a leg."

"You're making me feel uncomfortable." Tanya shifted slightly, her back against the cold of the driver's door. "Can you please just leave me alone?"

"I'm making *you* feel uncomfortable?" The man shook his head in disbelief. "I just need a jump start, I have the leads and everything." The man took a slight step toward Tanya.

"Hey, buddy," another man's voice said from the street.

Tanya turned her head slightly and could see someone crossing the road toward them. It was another stranger, but the sight of him made her sigh in relief.

"I think the lady has had enough, yeah? She told you she's feeling uncomfortable."

"But I—" the first man said.

"I heard what you said." The new stranger was now just a few feet away. "I think you'd best go back to your car and call that towing service that's going to bankrupt you."

The man in the hoodie looked at the girl, then at the other man, and started to back off.

"It was a simple request."

The other man was wearing a red baseball cap. Tanya thought he had a friendly smile beneath a graying mustache.

"I tell you what," he said. "How about I help you? You get your car started, the lady can feel safe, and we can all be on our way."

Tanya still didn't like the idea, but if it was going to defuse the situation, she felt it necessary. She often felt wracked with guilt, and if there was an option to help the man with the dead battery, then later on she wouldn't pick over whether she did the right or wrong thing by just leaving.

"Where are the leads?" the man in the red baseball cap asked.

"I'll get them," the man in the black hoodie said. He walked around to the rear of his car and opened the trunk.

"Thank you," Tanya whispered to the man in the red baseball cap. "I'm Tanya."

"No problem," he said quietly so the other man wouldn't hear him. "I'm Wallace."

There was another silence.

The man in the black hoodie was completely obscured by the open trunk.

"Why's he taking so long?" Wallace grumbled.

Tanya started to feel nervous again. The man in the hoodie had been rummaging around in the back of his car for far too long. She started to feel frightened. It was, to her at least, as if the man was back there contemplating something.

The trunk suddenly slammed shut and the man in the hoodie walked over with the jump leads. He handed them to Wallace.

"Great," Wallace said. "Now, Tanya, you pop the hood and we'll get this done."

Tanya opened her car door and pulled the open hood button, before crossing her arms by the driver's door. Wallace walked around and started to fumble with the leads, connecting them to Tanya's battery.

While he did, Tanya felt the pressing stare of the man in the black hoodie.

She smiled nervously at him, but he remained stone-faced.

"Okay!" Wallace said. "Now your turn, my friend."

The man in the hoodie walked slowly to the front of his car, popped the hood, and then attached the cables. Twice Tanya felt him glare momentarily at her. He made her skin crawl.

"Start her up," said Wallace.

The man in the hoodie sat in his car, turned the ignition, and his engine sputtered into life. Wallace then disconnected the leads from both cars and closed the hoods. He handed the leads back over to the driver through the open window.

"I guess you'll be on your way now, huh?" Wallace offered, jovially, but with a seriousness beneath.

"I just needed some help," the man said loudly so Tanya could hear.

"And now you have it. There's nothing else here for you," Wallace said sternly.

The man in the hoodie glared once more at Tanya. She was glad

Wallace was there. Those eyes, if that man had been alone with Tanya, she shivered to think what he might have done.

Finally, the man in the hoodie pulled away in his car. As he drove past Tanya he sneered at her through the window. And then he was gone.

Wallace fixed his cap and walked over to Tanya by her car.

"There ya go, young lady," he said.

"I can't thank you enough," she said, smiling.

"Oh, that's okay. You really need to be careful with creeps like that."

"Thanks for all your help, Wallace."

"No problem," he said. "But there is one thing you could do for me in return, if you don't mind?"

"Yes?"

Wallace pulled a large knife from his pocket and held it to Tanya's throat. "Get in the car or I'll cut you open and let you bleed out on the street."

Tanya felt the cold steel against her throat. For the first time in her life, she was acutely aware of the veins in her neck pulsing with blood, and how they could so easily by slit open. Death would follow in an instant.

"Wallace, please," Tanya said.

"Dumb as well as beautiful," the man said. "My name isn't Wallace. Any more than this mustache is real. Get in the car."

The man in the red baseball cap opened the door and threw Tanya inside her car. He hopped in alongside, pressing the blade against the side of her belly.

"Drive," he said. "And if you don't do exactly as I say, you'll be all over tomorrow's front pages. At least, pieces of you will be."

Terrified, her hands shaking, Tanya put the car into drive and drove slowly down the street, looking for a way out of the situation. Hoping she would see another day.

CHAPTER FIFTEEN

Valerie's eyes had adapted to the glare of the overhead lights. Darryl Minski's had not.

It was a little trick she liked to pull during questioning suspects in the interview room. Slowly have the lights ramped up in a way that makes the suspect squirm a little without knowing exactly why.

"I'm telling you, I did not kill those women," Darryl Minski said for what seemed like the fortieth time. His appointed defense lawyer sat beside him in a smart black suit.

"And we're supposed to believe that?" Charlie mocked from across the gray table of the interview room. It was covered in photographs found at Darryl's apartment. "Tell me, Darryl, if you were in our shoes, what would you believe?"

"I don't have to listen to any of this. You can keep asking all you want, you won't get anything from me."

"We know you stalked both victims, Darryl," Valerie said, pointedly. "You contacted both on social media, and you have photos of them. One looks suspiciously like it was taken while Shelly Bridges was hiking through George Washington and Jefferson National Forests."

"I'm not going to answer any of these questions." Darryl sounded dejected.

"You don't have to," the lawyer observed. "However…"

"However," Valerie continued, "we have more than enough to keep you here for stalking and harassment. So if you…"

There was a knock at the door.

"Excuse me," Valerie said. "Charlie."

Both agents left the room, leaving Darryl Minski and his lawyer beneath the glare of the interview room lights.

In the corridor outside, Jackson Weller and Will stood waiting.

"We've been watching through the glass," Jackson said, referring to the two-way mirror in the interview room. "You've been at it for hours, I don't think this guy is going to confess."

Valerie sighed. "Well, we have enough on him for stalking, so we charge him and keep him here at HQ for a little longer."

"Might I suggest something?" Will asked.

"Sure thing, Will," Charlie said.

"Could I speak with the suspect?"

"Yeah, you can come in with us." Valerie turned to open the door.

"No, I mean, alone, if that's okay?" Will said.

"Do you think we'd cramp your style, Doc?" Charlie asked.

"No, you're both doing great," he said. "But I think a change in tact might help. I have a theory about Darryl."

"And what's that?" Jackson sounded intrigued.

"I don't think he's the killer."

There was a silence for a moment. In that silence Valerie could feel it inside of her: The brewing doubt. She wanted Darryl to be guilty, but his personality was far removed from what was necessary to kill the victims so ruthlessly. Valerie was certain Darryl had trauma, trauma deep enough to pervert his mind and create an unsavory relationship with women in his mind, but not to the extent of murdering them.

There was also the question of distance... *Yes,* she thought. *Distance from the victims.* This thought was quickly interrupted.

"Why would you think that he isn't the killer, Will?" Charlie sounded a little annoyed.

"I've been profiling Darryl with everything we have on him," Will said, adjusting his glasses. "And listening to your interview, I don't think he fits."

"Valerie?" Jackson asked.

Valerie nodded with disappointment. "I've been having the same suspicions."

"Oh come on." Charlie sighed. "He's got to be the killer."

"No, Charlie," Valerie said. "Will is right. This guy likes to be at a distance from the girls. They are objects to document. He's fascinated by them. I don't think he wants to get too close to those objects in his mind."

"May I?" Will said, pointing to the door.

"Go for it," said Valerie. "We'll watch through the glass."

Valerie, Jackson, and Charlie moved through another door into a darkened room and watched through the soundproof glass as Will entered the interview room. His voice came through a speaker in the wall.

This was exciting to Valerie. She'd never really seen Will carry out a proper interview before. He was, however, used to talking to psychopaths after they had been caught, and he was known for his skill in getting information out from them.

Valerie watched, enthralled.

"My name is Doctor Will Cooper."

Darryl nodded.

"I'm not here to ask a question."

"What's he doing?" said Jackson, sounding worried.

"I don't know," Valerie replied, puzzled.

They continued to watch through the glass.

"Darryl," Will said, "when you were a young boy, you were chastised by your mother for showing interest in girls."

Darryl's eyes widened. "How... How do you know that?"

Will continued.

"By the time you were eleven, just before puberty, your fascination with women became sexual. But your mother was smothering. She forbid you to watch films or television programs showing women in an alluring way. This meant you were not exposed to the music videos and pop culture most of the other kids were."

"She said it was vile," Darryl said in a low voice.

"Puberty was a very difficult time for you," Will said. "Your mind was filled with fantasies about women, but you had a deep self-hatred for thinking that way. Your mother forbid it. And to give in to those fantasies would have meant admitting your mother was wrong."

"I... I don't understand," Darryl said, leaning into the table. "How... Who have you been speaking with?"

"Your file says you went to college," Will observed. "This is when your fascination for women, for your impulses, increased. But you had to keep your distance. You couldn't allow yourself to give in to those impulses. You couldn't so much as go on a date. You couldn't even have women friends. No, that was too risky. Your mother was right. Sexual thoughts were bad. You had to resist. But you found a loophole, didn't you, Darryl?"

"I don't know—"

"Darryl, you found that if you photographed women, it meant keeping that distance. You weren't betraying your mother, her moral crusade against sex, but you could explore your own urges this way. You could document, all the while staying distant. It made you feel power. Power you've never had. You were so close to the women. The objects of your desire. But you still felt pure. But if your mother ever found out..."

Darryl put his head in his hands and started sobbing.

"I didn't mean to hurt anyone," he said through the tears. "I just wanted to be close to them... God, I'm so messed up."

"Yes, you are," said Will. "But if it's worth anything. I don't think you're a killer. You have certain perversions. But those can be worked through with counseling and facing your crimes. I simply think you couldn't kill, because you don't hate them, do you?"

"No," he said. "I'm fascinated by them."

Will pointed to one of the photographs. It showed Shelly Bridges hiking through a woodland scene. "Where was this taken, Darryl?"

Finally, Darryl was giving in.

Valerie was impressed. "Will is good, I'll give him that."

But Will couldn't hear that. Not from the other side of the soundproof glass.

Darryl looked at the photograph. "It was taken on the Crying Wolf trail," he said quietly.

Will glanced to the mirror and then back. "On the day Shelly was murdered?"

Darryl nodded. "Yeah. It must have been."

"How did you know she'd be there?"

"I'd been gathering info about her online," Darryl answered. "Things she liked to do. I just wanted to know her more... Anyway, I was on a forum."

"Wild Trekking?" inquired Will.

"Yes, Doctor. I knew she was going to be trying that Crying Wolf trail and I got lucky. I had taken to sitting outside her apartment on Saturday mornings, because that was when she'd often go hiking. As I was following her, I figured out where she was going from the route."

"So you overtook and hid somewhere in the bushes along the trail," Will offered.

"Exactly. And that's how I got those shots. I swear that was all it was."

"It is a pretty big coincidence that you had photos of both Cassandra and Shelly," Will said.

"Not really," Darryl disagreed. "Shelly went to my college and Cassandra was always hanging about my neighborhood. That's how I kind of got to know them. Just online messages, though. And a couple of words on the street."

Valerie had heard enough. She and Charlie left the soundproofed room and reentered the interview.

Darryl looked up at Valerie as she walked in.

"Did you hear all that?" he asked. "In the movies, people are always behind that glass."

"Yeah, we heard," Valerie answered. "This doesn't quite get you off yet, Darryl. We can place you near where Shelly was murdered."

"No," Darryl said. "I had to leave just after I took those shots, my mother called and needed me. She ended up in the hospital."

"What time was this?" Charlie asked.

"About eight a.m."

"What time was the victim murdered?" the defense lawyer asked.

"A few hours later," Valerie mused before turning back to Darryl. "Did you visit your mother in the hospital?"

"Yes!" Darryl said, realizing the implication. "I went there right away, got there about nine a.m. The nurses will remember me! And I should be on the CCTV."

"We'll check that out," Valerie said. "But even if you're telling the truth, you're still being charged with stalking."

Another knock came at the door.

Valerie sighed. "All these interruptions."

She moved to the door and opened it.

It was Jackson, and he looked as grim as he ever had.

"What's happened?" Valerie asked.

"The *Chronicle* is about to run with a story. They say they have a letter from the killer. And if he follows through on his threats, there's going to be a bloodbath."

CHAPTER SIXTEEN

This was the third time Valerie had been to the offices of the *Washington Chronicle* on M Street in DC, but never with this much at stake.

She now sat alongside Charlie in the office of Mark Williams, the editor of the *Washington Chronicle*. Valerie had spoken with Williams before, and he wore his anti-FBI feelings on his sleeve for all to see.

He was proud of being anti-establishment.

Valerie sympathized with those who were suspicious of power—she was too—and she was glad there were people always willing to call out abuses of power, but when it came to catching a brutal killer, that was her only goal.

Will had been called away to attend to one of his therapy patients. Given his amazing performance with Darryl Minski, she had hoped he would be with them now. But it wasn't possible. She only used his skills sparingly, whenever she had them at her disposal.

But she understood. Will had patients, he had people who needed him.

"Can we see it?" Charlie asked.

"Oh," said Williams, rubbing the stubble on his chin and grinning. "Now this is a first. The FBI aren't usually this cordial with us."

"Time is of the essence, Mr. Williams," Valerie said. "We need to know what the killer's intentions are. Jackson Weller said his source told him briefly that there was a threat to kill again."

"His source?" Williams thumped his closed fist onto his desk. "I knew there was a snitch in this office. I'll weed them out."

"It could have come from the postal service," Charlie said, clearly hoping to diffuse William's suspicions.

The editor shook his head. "No, I've suspected for some time there's a weasel among us. Do you know who it is?"

"I don't," said Valerie. "But you know that even if I did, I couldn't tell you."

Williams grinned maliciously. "Well, maybe I just can't tell you what's in that letter, either. You can read it like everyone else in tomorrow's edition." He sat back down in a brown leather office chair that swung back slightly.

"I can't stop you from publishing the letter," said Valerie. "But you would be impeding a federal investigation if you don't at least let us read it."

"I'll take my chances." Williams rummaged around in a drawer of his desk and pulled out a cigar. "You mind if I smoke?"

"I do," said Valerie.

Williams grinned and lit the cigar anyway, blowing smoke rings into the air. The air conditioning above eventually got hold of the rings, pulled them apart, and sucked them up into the unseen veins of the building.

Valerie knew she could get a warrant to see the letter. But every minute without that information was another minute the killer had to find another victim. She took a different approach instead.

"You know, Williams," she said, "Jackson's source told him some other tidbits from around the office. Especially regarding your use of company funds to pay for hotel rooms. For you and one of your employees."

"How is your wife, by the way?" Charlie said, smiling.

Valerie hated the veiled threat, and it was one she and Charlie would never follow through on, but innocent women's lives were at stake, and she wasn't about to let a newspaper editor put his grandstanding before their safety.

Williams's demeanor quickly changed. He grumbled and then rested his cigar on a white marble ashtray and looked at the two FBI agents.

Valerie felt as though she were being sized up. Would he refuse? Were they capable of releasing information that could be damaging to him?

Valerie stared right back. She didn't flinch. She didn't blink.

Finally, the editor grinned again. "Okay, I see how it is," he said.

Williams stood up and went over to a cabinet on the wall that had a few whiskey bottles resting on it. He opened the cabinet revealing a safe. Inside the safe was a brown envelope.

"Here," he said, returning to his desk. "Take it. We'd have had to hand it over to authorities anyway after publication, and we have a copy."

Valerie put on a pair of white latex gloves from her pocket and opened the envelope. When she pulled it out, she was amazed at how rudimentary it was. The killer had cut up letters from newspapers and magazines and used those letters to write.

"He's smart," said Charlie. "A good way not to get caught. We have no handwriting to analyze. But can we be sure it's not a fake?"

Reading the letter out loud, Valerie's stomach lurched. It was real.

"*People are cattle*," she read. "*I killed two such cattle in recent days. One of them had a burn on the inside of her leg.*"

Charlie sighed. "Well, that seals it. We didn't release that to the public."

"She was on the Crying Wolf trail, but I was the wolf," Valerie continued. "I waited. I stalked. And I slit her open. But look what I did. She's on the news. I made her famous. She would thank me."

"Sick son of a—" Williams offered, showing at least some humanity.

Valerie continued until the last sentence of the letter, pausing for a moment.

Williams's eyes lit up. "That last line is something else, ain't it?"

"What does it say?" Charlie asked.

Valerie cleared her throat. She hated to read the man's words. They were his works, and she now knew his works well. They were forged in steel and blood.

"It says… *I will cut them up like animals. In your parks. Yours schools. Your homes. No one will be safe. I will come for your mothers, your sisters, and your daughters. And you will all know my name…. Yours in blood, the Bone Ripper.*"

"The Bone Ripper?" asked Charlie. "That's what he's calling himself?"

"Quite a name, eh?" Williams said, seemingly taking delight in it.

Valerie could sense the editor's love of a good story. The Bone Ripper would sell papers, that was for sure.

"You think he got the name Ripper from Jack the Ripper?" Charlie asked.

"Seems possible," Valerie mused. "But then, going by the brutal way that the victims have been opened up and bones broken and cut in places, it's possible he's referring to that."

Williams phone rang on his desk.

"Hello?" he said. "I see. Okay. Send Icho over."

He put the phone back down, ending the call.

Charlie was now studying the letter, but Valerie was studying something else. She was watching Williams. For the first time since they'd entered the room he looked restless.

His fingers were tapping on his desk and he was looking around a little too much.

"Something wrong, Williams?" Valerie asked.

"No, not at all," he said. "Not at all."

Now it was Valerie's turn to be notified. A notification buzzed on her phone. It was from HQ.

Another victim. Call Jackson immediately.

Valerie felt her heart sink. They hadn't been fast enough. Another woman had been brutally butchered by the Bone Ripper, as he called himself.

She leaned over and showed Charlie the message.

"Damn," was all he could say.

Williams was watching the agents.

"Well," he said leaning back in his chair, "if you know what I know, looks like we have sources of our own, too." He grinned.

Valerie didn't take the bait. She and Charlie left and headed immediately to the crime scene.

CHAPTER SEVENTEEN

Valerie and Charlie walked across the deserted field, the moonless sky casting no shadows. They were only guided by the beams of their flashlights, and the flashing red and blue lights out there in the black void.

A patrolman came out of the darkness, buttoned up for the colder weather right up to his chin.

"Agents Law, Carlson," the man said. "I'm glad you're here."

"Thank you," Valerie replied in kind. "Can you show us the body?"

"This way," the officer said, moving across the field. "Watch your step, a lot of this is uneven."

The low-cut grass bobbed in the night breeze as Valerie's flashlight caught a set of two tire tracks. She could see where the tracks led, straight from the nearest road in the distance to a point in the middle of the field. A car sat where the tracks terminated, and something was hanging out through the passenger window.

"My God, is that the victim?" Charlie asked. "Christ, this is worse than Shelly Bridges."

Valerie agreed, though she didn't say it. The body was of a woman in her late twenties. Using her flashlight, Valerie lit up the true horror of the scene.

The woman had been tied up with thin metal chains. Her hands were bound, and they had been lashed to the frame of the car through a smashed hole in the windshield. She was facing down with her body hanging out of the passenger window, the door still closed.

Casting the beam of her flashlight into the interior of the car, Valerie could see the woman's legs lying in the driver's seat.

"The killer amputated her legs, looks like with a saw," Valerie said, her voice almost trembling. "The woman then just bled out."

"It's unbelievable," the patrolman said. "I've never seen anything like this."

"Me neither," said Valerie. "At least not in person."

"Look here," Charlie noted. "On the back of her neck. He's engraved something. Looks like the words Bone Ripper. Right into her skin."

"And here on her mouth, Charlie. Looks like gag marks. He must have gagged her with something to keep her screaming down while he… cut."

Charlie shone his flashlight on the ground around the car.

"I don't see any gag," he said. "It's missing. A trophy, maybe?"

"Could be."

Valerie stepped away to gather her thoughts. She took a few steps across the grass and turned her back on the vehicle.

Charlie was by her side.

"Are you okay?" he asked.

Valerie nodded. But she was far from okay. Whenever she chased down a killer, she beat herself up inside. Once she was on the case, she took responsibility for subsequent deaths. She always blamed herself for not catching the killer sooner.

"She's about the age of my sister," Valerie said in hushed tones.

It was the chains. Valerie saw them around the dead woman's hands, and it could only make her think of how Suzie was tied up in the psychiatric hospital. For a moment, she thought she heard her sister's voice coming from the darkness.

Help me, it said. But it was in her mind. It had to be.

"Val," Charlie said softly. "I know you've got a lot on with family at the moment. If this is too much, just say and we'll—"

"I'm fine." Valerie turned, her voice strong. She looked over Charlie's shoulder. "Who the hell is this?"

Two men were clambering across the field.

"Ah, shit," one of them said, wearing a long raincoat. "They got here first. I told you we took a wrong turn!"

"We're here now," the other man said, pulling out a camera and taking snaps of the car as they approached.

The patrolman was busily trying to stop them from getting any closer, but it wasn't until Charlie and Valerie ran over that the two intruders stopped in their tracks.

"I take it you're Icho?" Valerie asked the man in the long coat.

"Ha," he said. "Agent Law, I presume. Williams said you'd be here."

"Well, Icho, as a reporter, what do you want to know?" Charlie stood, looming over the rest of the group.

"Is this the third victim of the Bone Ripper?"

The photographer tried to take a step around Charlie to get a clearer

77

shot of the car and body, but Charlie grabbed him by the arm and pushed him back. "Let's not have a disagreement, now. I wouldn't want to get unfriendly with the press."

"You're not going to impede our documenting of this, are you?" Icho snapped.

"No," Valerie said. "Just like you're not going to impede our active crime scene. Feel free to get closer. But I will arrest you on the spot for contaminating a murder scene."

Icho tried to look over Valerie's shoulder for a moment. He then turned to the photographer.

"Did you get a shot?" he asked.

"Yeah, one, I think. It's grainy. But it'll do."

Icho nodded and then smiled. "Let's be friends, Agent Law. You scratch my back and I'll scratch yours. You answer a few questions about the case, and I'll promise to bring anything I get through unofficial channels to you right away. Can't say fairer than that?" He stretched his hand out.

Valerie thought it out for a moment. She knew it would prove useful to have a reporter with his ear to the ground. The FBI had informants, they had the wide network of law enforcement up and down the country, but even that net had holes in it. Besides, she knew she could give him just enough without really breaching protocol.

"Okay, agreed," Valerie said, shaking his hand.

"Deal," Icho replied, looking her in the eye. "We'll back off to the road over there and then when you're done here, we can have a short interview, if that's cool?"

"Sure," Valerie said as Icho and his photographer walked back off the field.

"Do you think it's wise to speak with the press?" Charlie quietly asked.

"Better to have some control over the info, Charlie. Who knows, he and the *Chronicle* might end up giving us something useful."

Charlie turned back to the horrific scene behind. The murder victim's body was still in the same position, lying through the passenger window.

"Call our forensics team, get them down here right away, Charlie."

"Will do," Charlie said, taking out his cell phone. He then looked over at the patrolman. "Officer, who found the body?"

"A local farmer," the officer replied. "He was coming back from a bar in the nearest town, and he saw the tracks going into his field. But he didn't see anything other than that."

"We'll question him in the morning," Valerie said. "Make some inquiries and see if there's any security footage of the victim and her car before the murder. Right now, I've got an interview to do."

Valerie walked across the field toward where Icho and the photographer were. She found them by the side of a country road.

Icho smiled like a carnival owner, taking out a small H1 audio recorder.

Valerie would give him just enough to make him happy, she knew that. But it would be difficult for her to cover up the truth: She was at a dead end. The killer was out there and there were no leads.

Somewhere in the darkness across the road in another field, something moved near a small stream. *Just one more animal*, Valerie thought. *The world is full of them.*

Sunrise would come soon enough, and it would bring with it the most difficult of tasks. Valerie would look for the victim's loved ones, and hope beyond hope that someone had seen the killer before he so mercilessly took another victim's life.

CHAPTER EIGHTEEN

Valerie carried three photos in her hands. They felt heavy. They felt precious. They felt disgusting.

The photographs were the first proper lead they'd found on the case, and Valerie knew that they were her lifeline. Her avenue to catching the sadistic Bone Ripper before he killed again.

Where she carried these photographs to, now that wore heavily on her heart. Because she was about to show them to the third victim's husband.

Two officers stood on the porch of a small town house as Valerie approached. Charlie and Will were by her side.

Will stopped for a moment as they walked up through the lush garden, an array of beautiful shrubs and flowers spreading out around an immaculate lawn. Will looked at the flowers.

"You say she was a florist, Valerie?" he said.

"Yes."

"I wonder…"

"What's on your mind, Will?" asked Charlie.

"Sometimes when interviewing serial killers, I come across what I label 'oppositional motives.' I was just wondering if that applied here."

Valerie knew Will had contributed to several textbooks when she was training as an agent.

"So, you think the fact that she was a florist might have something to do with it?" Valerie asked.

"Possibly. Possibly not," Will answered, running his fingers over a delicate purple flower. "I just think it's interesting to think that the victim was involved in beauty, and beauty provided by the rich flowers of the earth. I wonder if the killer wanted to sully that. To snuff that out. He may be motivated by the opposite of what he does. He may want to wipe beauty from the world. Tanya Brenning was someone who gave beauty to the world."

Valerie was glad for Will's insight. It wasn't always the correct path, but his way of thinking added something to the investigation. He brainstormed ideas about profiles and motivations in a way that no agent she knew of could. Even Charlie, and he had a brilliant mind.

Will looked up from the flower and then to the house at the end of the garden, the two police officers still waiting on the white porch.

"Are you okay, Valerie?" he said.

Valerie was sideswiped by this. *What does he mean? Does he know I'm struggling? Does he know my fears? Is he profiling me?*

"I'm fine, Will," she answered, trying to sound confident. But the pain of her sister's deterioration had wounded her deeply. Just early that morning she had received a call about another incident at the psychiatric hospital. Suzie had tried to attack one of the orderlies.

How long before that's me in there? This thought clouded Valerie's judgment. She had to be rid of it. At least for now.

"I'm fine, Will," Valerie restated. "Why?"

"You look tired," Will said. "And I've noticed you seem a bit preoccupied."

He's too good, Valerie thought. *If I start to lose my mind like my mom and sister, he'll know.*

"Just haven't been sleeping great," Valerie said.

"You know," Charlie interrupted, "we could do this bit ourselves, Val. If you wanted? I know how much it hurts to do this, and if you're feeling a bit…"

"I'm fine, Charlie. Honestly. I'm just thinking about the case. That's all."

"Okay," Charlie said, unconvincingly.

Valerie tried to calm herself and focus on the case, to focus on a different type of discomfort. Pain was indeed up ahead, because she now had to speak with Tanya's husband, a man who had just lost his wife under the most horrific of circumstances.

*

Harry Brenning sat in the immaculate living room of his town house, once a place he was building a life with his wife, Tanya. His hands were shaking, his face pale and drawn. He looked, to Valerie at least, like someone who had been suddenly given a terminal diagnosis.

But grief was a kind of a death. This Valerie knew. It was never just the victim who was lost after a violent death. Something died inside their loved ones, too.

"Can I get you some water, Mr. Brenning?" Valerie asked.

"No. No, thank you," he said. "I still can't believe this."

81

"It'll take time," Charlie offered. "We'll put you in touch with a bereavement counselor if you'd like. That can really help you through the grieving process."

Harry Brenning looked up. He scanned the faces of Valerie, then Charlie, and then Will. He stopped at Will.

"I know you," he said. "I remember seeing you on a couple of documentaries about serial killers."

"Yes, Mr. Brenning, I've been asked to be in a few," Will said.

"So... So I'm guessing whoever did this to Tanya," Mr. Brenning said through tears, "that he's killed before, if you're here as an expert?"

"That's right," Valerie answered. "And we're going to do everything we can to catch him."

"I'd tear his throat out," Mr. Brenning said through gritted teeth. "Tanya was so sweet, she didn't deserve this."

"Mr. Brenning," asked Charlie, "do you know of any enemies Tanya might have had?"

"No. I can genuinely say everyone loved her."

"And what about strange behavior?" Will inquired.

"Strange behavior?" Mr. Brenning repeated.

"Yes," Valerie continued. "Anyone hanging around her store, or unwanted messages, anything like that?"

"No. Nothing she told me about."

Valerie pointed to the photographs in her hands. "Would you mind looking at these to see if it sparks a memory?"

"Is it him? Do you have photos?"

"We think so," Valerie answered. "And a witness. Tanya was asked by a man to help her jump-start his car. We identified him like we did Tanya, through his registration plate. He said another man came along and helped. A security camera from a storefront captured the second man pulling out a knife and getting into the car with Tanya."

"I want to see him," Mr. Brenning said, his voice filled with anger. "I want to see his face."

Valerie laid the photographs out on the table. They were grainy. But Valerie had had them enhanced as best as possible back at the Mesmer Building. One of them was a close-up, showing a man in a baseball cap with a mustache

Mr. Brenning held the photo up and glared at it. He then put it down and sobbed.

"You don't know him?" said Charlie.

Mr. Brenning only shook his head.

"This photo will be going out on local news and in the *Chronicle*, as well as some smaller papers," Valerie informed Mr. Brenning. "It might be best to avoid these things for now."

Mr. Brenning looked up.

"But how will I know if you find him?"

"You'd be the first to know," Valerie said reassuringly. She felt so sorry for the man. His life was in ruins because of the killer. She just hoped that Mr. Brenning would be able to find peace eventually.

That wasn't always the outcome. Some tended toward self-destruction and being devoured with unanswered questions. Did they feel anything at the end? Were they awake? Did they shout a loved one's name?

Valerie pushed those thoughts from her mind. They were sometimes too difficult to bear. And she had a job to do.

"We'll do everything we can to find him," Valerie said, standing up. "And if there's anything that comes to mind, anything that might help us, here's my card."

Mr. Brenning took the card. He said "Thank you" in a low voice and then disappeared into another room.

Charlie, Valerie, and Will walked out onto the porch and then into the yard so no one else could hear.

"Thoughts, Charlie, Will?"

"It's a disguise," Charlie said. "The killer has been so careful this far."

"But killers become less careful as they're consumed by their blood lust," Will said.

"It doesn't feel like he's enraged," Valerie said. "He's under control. To have amputated Tanya's legs like that to let her bleed out when someone could have come along. This is someone who is methodical."

"I think we should run a search for medical professionals in the area with a criminal record," suggested Will. "The man must have medical knowledge."

"But it's too haphazard to be a doctor, in my opinion," Valerie mused. "Someone with basic anatomy experience could have done this."

"The *Chronicle* is running their story this morning," Charlie added. He held up his phone with a digital copy.

The headline read "Bone Ripper Claims Third Victim."

"What did you tell Icho in your interview, Val?"

"He asked if it was the third victim," Val replied. "I didn't say at that point, though obviously we know the killer engraved his new nickname into the back of Tanya's neck. I was hoping to keep that out of the press for now. It would be a way for the killer to identify he did it during a confession."

"I had another look at the letter the *Chronicle*'s editor passed on to you," Will said, pushing his glasses up his nose, which Valerie knew invariably meant a theory was coming.

"Anything new in your analysis?" Charlie prodded.

"Just something to add to the profile," Will said. "I think the killer is desperate to be known. He wants to feel big by going as large as he can with these killings. That would suggest to me that he's making up for some inadequacy in his life."

"I agree," said Valerie. "The killer wants to be famous. He wants to be known. That must mean he doesn't have that validation from elsewhere. It's a good anchor point to the profile, Will. But we still don't know much about why he feels a need for validation."

"Overbearing parents," said Charlie as an option. "Sexual inadequacy, not being seen romantically by others, career failure, financial bankruptcy, a bad father; there are any number of ways he might feel inadequate in his life."

"What it does give us," Valerie pointed out, "is a motive of sorts. He wants to be famous or infamous. That means he's going to go larger with each kill. And he's going to court the press. We can expect more letters."

Valerie let out a loud sigh. She rubbed her eyes.

"Are you okay, Val?" Charlie asked.

She looked up. "I wish people would stop asking that! I'm fine!"

There was a slow silence.

"Sorry, Charlie," she said. "I'm just exhausted."

"It's a couple of hours' drive back to Quantico from here," Will observed. "Might we stay in a motel somewhere, get some rest and back to it in the morning?"

"I'll let my wife know I won't be home," Charlie said.

Valerie didn't argue. She was shattered. The case. Her sister and mom on her mind.

Sleep, I need sleep, she thought, walking back to the car, her mind in a daze.

CHAPTER NINETEEN

Valerie woke groggily. It took her a moment to open her eyes. They felt like they were being pulled down by lead weights.

The room in which she found herself was familiar. To a professional like Valerie, she'd seen the inside of a psychiatric hospital room many times before. Visiting her sister Suzie recently, she'd seen enough of them outside of work, too.

But never from this position. Never while dressed in a hospital gown.

Valerie's pulse raced.

Where am I? she thought. *How did I end up in here?*

She closed her eyes and shook her head, but it did nothing to remove the fog in her mind. The memory was hazy. Something bad had happened. Something she had done herself.

The door opened and a pale woman with short black hair and glasses entered the room, carrying a clipboard.

"Good morning, Valerie," the woman said. "How are you feeling this morning?"

"Who are you?" Valerie said. "Where am I? What's going on?"

"I'm Dr. Grimes," the woman said. "You're at Compton Hills Psychiatric Hospital. You've been here for two days now."

"What happened?" Valerie said.

"You don't remember?" the doctor asked.

"I…" Valerie said.

"You don't remember what happened or you don't remember being here?" the doctor said.

"A little of both, I guess… I'm an FBI agent. I was working on a case." She tried to sit up, but her body ached and her head throbbed.

"You were shot," the doctor said. "Three times, actually. It's amazing you're still alive. The paramedics said they couldn't believe it. We did multiple surgeries to try to help you, but I have to be honest: I didn't think you'd make it."

"What happened after I was shot?" Valerie said.

"You were in a coma for two days," the doctor said. "But you were

85

starting to come out of it a couple of days ago."

"Oh." Valerie felt utterly drained and confused. She tried to remember, but she couldn't. She pushed through her mind with all her will, but there was nothing there. It was a black void of nothingness.

"But this isn't a normal hospital, it's a psychiatric hospital room. The walls are padded so I don't bash my brains off of them. Why am I here?"

The doctor nodded. "Yes, I'm afraid you had a psychotic break."

Those words stuck in Valerie's heart like a thorn. Especially the word "break."

So, it's finally happened, she thought. *I've gone mad like my sister and mother.*

"Where's Charlie and Will?" Valerie asked, finally finding the strength to sit up and pull her feet onto the floor.

"Charlie is in the hospital, Valerie. He'll survive. But I'm afraid to say that Will did not. He was shot point-blank in the heart."

Valerie felt dizzy. She felt sick. Her friend, her colleague, had been murdered.

She started to cry.

"Was it the Bone Ripper?"

"Bone Ripper?" the doctor repeated. "Oh no, Valerie. It was *you*."

Those words stopped her dead.

"No... That's impossible!" Valerie screamed.

"I'm afraid you thought he was a serial killer and you went into a murderous rage. He tried to talk you out of holding the gun. He nearly succeeded. But you shot him anyway. How does that make you feel?"

Valerie wanted out. She wanted out of the room. Out of the hospital. Out of this nightmare.

Standing up, she yelled: "I would never do that!"

But even though those words came from her mouth, she doubted them.

Yes, you could. You could have done it. Just like Mom cut you without being in her right mind. Just like Suzie growing violent. It's the sickness. It's the family sickness.

"No..." she said through tears.

"Charlie had to shoot you," the doctor said, sighing. "It will take him quite a while to get over that, I'm sure."

"None of this makes any sense! I don't believe you!"

"Calm down. I think it's time for your medication, Valerie," the doctor said.

The door to the room opened and a man in a white orderly uniform stepped in. He handed a syringe to the doctor.

The man looked at Valerie, and there was something about him. The way he stood, the slight smile that was creeping around the corner of his mouth. His dead, sunken eyes.

"No," Valerie said. "This isn't possible."

"What's wrong, Valerie?" the doctor asked.

Valerie pointed to the orderly with the syringe. "That man is Arthur Harlow, and he's dead!"

"Well, dear, his name is Arthur, but not Harlow, and he is very much alive," the doctor explained. "He's probably just entered into your delusion. You mustn't fixate on these things. Now, why don't you let me give you this medicine."

Arthur handed the syringe to the doctor.

"No!" Valerie yelled. "That man *is* Arthur Harlow. A killer. He killed several people a few months ago and he died during the arrest. It can't be him!"

"Hold her down, Arthur," the doctor said.

Arthur lunged forward and pinned Valerie to the bed. He seemed to have inhuman strength.

"Let me go!" Valerie screamed. Arthur's grip on her arms was agonizing

The doctor stepped forward.

"It's for your own good, Valerie," she said, sticking the syringe into Valerie's arm.

The doctor then turned without saying another word and left the room.

Arthur remained over Valerie staring down at her.

Valerie felt clouded. Whatever was in the syringe was working.

"Leave me... alone..."

"Like you left me alone?" Arthur whispered. "Or my brother?" He leaned in and stuck out his tongue, running it up her face. "I can taste it, Agent Law. Your fear. Now you're just another nut in the nuthouse like the rest of us."

Valerie suddenly felt paralyzed.

Arthur stood back and walked to the door. He then turned back to look at Valerie.

"Me and you are going to have a lot of time together in this place, Agent Law. Oh, and the Clawstitch Killer? He's here to. He sends his best. Welcome to your new home."

Arthur stepped out and the door slammed shut.

The drugs kicked in and Valerie passed out in a swirl of fear and confusion.

Valerie jumped as the door to her motel room broke open. Running through it were Charlie and Will, both looking disheveled as if woken abruptly from their sleep.

Charlie looked around the room as if scanning it for an unknown assailant.

"Are you okay?" Will asked, softly, stepping over to Valerie's bedside.

"I'm fine. I'm fine," Valerie said. "Close the door."

Charlie closed the door to the outside and messed around with the handle.

"I'll pay for that," Charlie said. Finally he managed to get it to shut.

Valerie gathered her thoughts as she pulled on some clothes. Charlie and Will turned their backs.

Valerie was horrified. The dream. The fear of being in a psychiatric ward. The appearance of Arthur Harlow from a previous case. It all came back to her.

And she had the sense that she had been screaming in her sleep.

"You can turn around now, guys," she said.

Charlie and Will turned to look at their friend and colleague.

"I'm sorry," Valerie said. "I was having a bad dream."

"A bad dream?" Charlie repeated. "It sounded like you were being murdered in here, Val."

A knock came at the door.

"Is everything all right?" the muffled voice of the motel manager said from outside.

Valerie walked over to the door. She opened it and showed her badge.

"Everything is fine, sir. Just a misunderstanding. We'll pay for the damage to the door."

The man seemed more unnerved by the FBI badge than anything else, and so he scuttled away back toward the seedy reception desk where he had been watching late-night TV.

"What's going on, Val?" Charlie said, his face etched with concern.

"Nothing," Valerie said. "I just have some things on my mind. The case and some other things. But I'm fine. Really."

Valerie was anything but fine underneath. Beneath that cool exterior that she wore so well was her own concern. The concern that she was developing a delusional mind, one that would start in her dreams and then seep out into her waking life. She started to panic inside, and her breathing became more staggered.

"I'm starting to get worried about you, Val," Charlie said. "You know, this case isn't worth all this."

Will put his arm around Valerie's shoulder.

"Would you like a hot drink?" he said in a fatherly tone. "You know what I always drink when I have a bad dream at night?"

"No," Valerie said, sitting on a couch.

"I have a nice soothing cup of chamomile tea," Will said with a kind smile. "I'm sure you've had it before, but you might not have known that chamomile is an old herbal medicine that's been used for thousands of years. And sometimes the ancients really did know best."

Valerie felt herself calming down just by the sound of Will's voice. "That sounds nice."

"Charlie, there's a hot drinks machine outside the reception," Will said. "I had a cup of chamomile from it myself before bed. Would you mind getting one for Valerie?"

"Not at all," Charlie said, and left the room.

Will pulled up a chair and sat in front of Valerie. He held her hand affectionately. If it had been anyone else, she would have thought they were putting a move on her. But not Will. Although he was only in early middle age, he felt like a kind uncle the way he held her hand. And in that moment, Valerie felt how she had missed out on having a dad or other father figure around to comfort her when she was going through her mother's breakdown as a kid.

"Valerie," Will said in soothing tones. "I've seen something in you since I've met you. Do you want to know what I see?"

Valerie was scared to say yes. She feared deeply that he sensed she was unhinged, or becoming so.

She didn't answer.

"I see," Will continued, "a kind, insightful, talented profiler. I see a brilliant FBI agent. I see someone devoted to helping others. I see someone who will do anything to stop brutal killers from tearing down the fabric of people's lives."

Valerie was taken aback. She and Will had grown close since their first case, but she had no idea he held her in such high esteem.

"Thank you," was all Valerie said.

"I also see," Will went on, "a beautiful person carrying the weight of the world on her shoulders. A beautiful person who has... a history

89

of deep trauma. I remember when you tried to talk Arthur Harlow down. How you mentioned your mother. I see it every now and then in your eyes. In your demeanor. You still carry that pain. And I suspect whatever is going on with your sister right now is bringing that pain to light once more."

"You see all that?" Valerie said, not knowing why he wouldn't. Will was a brilliant mind in the world of forensic psychology. Why should she not be read just as well by him as any killer?

"I do, Valerie. I do see it. And if you need to talk with someone I will always be here."

Those words "always be here" struck a nerve. She had never had an "always be here," not in a parental sense. Not someone looking out for her. She had always been the one looking out for others. Her kid sister. The public. Her partner.

Valerie pulled her hand away, gently. She rubbed her eyes as Charlie came back into the room.

"You know I care about you two," she said. "And I know you want to help, but please don't push on this. If I want to open up, I will."

Charlie handed the cup of chamomile tea over to her.

"I know, Val."

"And please, Charlie… you too, Will, please don't worry about my ability to handle the job right now. I can do it. Don't tell Jackson I'm having issues."

"We won't," said Will.

"Val," said Charlie, "I won't say anything. But you know you're family. If I think things are getting too much for you, I will intervene to keep you and us safe."

Valerie's heart sank. Yes, she knew this of Charlie. He'd always do what was best for her, even if it meant going against her wishes.

"I understand," she said. "But it'll be fine. Let's just catch us a killer. That's all we need to be worrying about."

Valerie smiled.

Her two friends and colleagues smiled back. But she could see it in their eyes.

They were not convinced.

She now knew she'd have to hide her fears of her deteriorating mind even more now. If she didn't, she would soon find herself off the case and, perhaps, out of the FBI.

CHAPTER TWENTY

Valerie stood as she had done many times before: arms crossed in front of the evidence board at HQ in Quantico, staring at the photographs of the killer's victims and wishing she could find something that would give her a new line of inquiry.

Jackson Weller was standing beside her while Charlie was at the back of the room working through his own notes.

"I don't want to put more pressure on you, Agent Law," Jackson said, quietly.

Valerie turned to Jackson. "That normally means you're going to anyway. Hit me with it."

Jackson looked uncomfortable, which was always a bad sign.

"Valerie," he said, "the higher-ups are now linking your performance in this case to what happened with the Clawstitch Killer."

That angered Valerie. They had no right. What had happened on the Clawstitch Killer case years ago was a bad moment, but she shouldn't have been tarred by it forevermore.

"Because I haven't caught the Bone Ripper yet?"

"It's more that you don't even have a profile, Valerie." Jackson leaned in. "I've vouched for you, and they're not talking about removing you, but every time he kills, it's more bad press for the Bureau. That's not your fault. And I disagree with their assessment. But you should know there's talk of bringing in outside assistance to the Criminal Psychopathy Unit if things don't start to look up soon."

"Other agents?" Valerie did not hide her disappointment.

"I'm doing my best to keep them off your back," Jackson said. "But we need something. Now. Put all your attention on it. I believe in you." He patted her on the back and left the room.

"Sounds like a lot of bureaucratic trash," Charlie said, having been listening in from the back of the room. "Don't let it get to you, Val. We'll have a breakthrough."

"I hope so…"

Charlie was grinning.

"Why are you smiling?"

"Well, I wasn't just at the back of the room sucking my thumb."

"Have you found something?" Suddenly Valerie felt a surge of hope in her bones.

"Yeah, I found something," Charlie said. "I ran a database search for convicted stalkers to see if any were released just before the first victim was killed."

"And?"

"I found one that might fit the bill, but I don't know. I have his file."

"Put it up on the touchscreen," Valerie said.

Moments later, the file was up on a large flat touchscreen that worked as a digital portal for Valerie when looking through files. She ran her finger across the screen and began reading.

She looked at the man's rap sheet. He was forty-eight years old and had done time twice for stalking behavior. Each time, he'd escalated his crimes. The last time, he'd followed a woman to her home, broken inside, and taken photos of her while she slept. He was caught leaving the scene by a neighbor

"What do you think?" Charlie asked.

"It could be," Valerie said, excitedly. "It's doubtful that he started killing out of the blue, but I don't see anything in his file that—"

"What is it?" Charlie asked.

"One of the women this perp stalked," Valerie pointed out. "She was into hiking, and he followed her to a remote location to take photos. She saw him and made it home, but the parallels with what happened to Shelly Bridges are striking."

"I'll call Will and see if he's available today," Charlie said.

"Yeah, we should have him with us in case he sees something we don't."

Valerie stared at the touchscreen as Charlie made the call to Will. She looked at the photo.

Is it you? she thought. *Are you the Bone Ripper?*

"Okay, Will's in," Charlie said, grabbing his keys. "Let's roll."

*

Valerie slammed her fist on the apartment door as Will and Charlie stood to the side in the hallway of the run-down apartment complex.

"Valerie, slow down," Charlie said. But she was in no mood to move slowly. It was only a matter of time before a fourth woman lost her life to that maniac.

"FBI. Open up," Valerie commanded.

"FBI?" the scared voice of a man said from the other side of the door. "What do you want?"

"We're here to question you about the murder of three women," Valerie said, loudly.

"This is the wrong play," Will whispered to Charlie.

Valerie heard this, but she knew she had to push through. They wanted to knock politely and question the man, but Valerie wasn't about to do this so nicely.

She used the images of the three victims in her mind to spur her on. Will and Charlie, for all their experience, were men. Valerie knew they couldn't understand. They could never truly know what it was like to live as a woman and to fear for your safety in countless instances across your life.

Valerie knew. To her, all women did.

"Open up now or I'm taking the door off the hinges," Valerie said, grimly.

"Okay, okay," the voice said. "I don't want any trouble."

The door opened, revealing the face of a man with gray-blond hair that fell past his shoulders and a large bald spot on the top of his head. He looked tired, and his eyes were wide and frightened.

He looked pitiful to Valerie. But she tried to bat away any sympathy. The killer had shown no pity for anyone else, so why should she if this really was the man?

Valerie put her foot forward so the man couldn't close the door.

"Mr. Kendrick? Alan Kendrick?" Charlie said, stepping alongside Valerie. He spoke in less harsh tones, clearly trying to deescalate the conversation.

"Yes… That's me," the man said timidly. "What's this about murdered women? The ones in the newspapers?"

The mention of newspapers piqued Valerie's interest. *Yes, the newspapers, the place you've been sending letters.*

"Could we come in and have a chat about this?" Charlie said quietly.

Alan Kendrick looked around fearfully and then bowed his head. He stepped back and let the three investigators into his home.

The apartment was minimalist at best. There was barely any furniture to speak of. Valerie saw a bedroom as she passed an open door. Only a bed and a few books were there. Clothes strewn across the floor.

The living room wasn't much better. An old brown couch with duct tape covering holes in the arms sat across from small flat-screen TV.

Alan Kendrick turned around once they were all in the room.

"Please don't tell me you think I murdered those poor women?" he said, his face etched with worry.

"You feel empathy for them?" Valerie asked.

"Of course!" Alan sat down on the couch shaking his head. "I know I did bad stuff in the past, but I—"

"You were released from prison days before the first victim was found," Valerie said coldly. "Given your track record, this is a bit of a coincidence, is it not?"

"No! I wouldn't do that," Alan said. "When I was arrested it was for taking pictures."

"And breaking into a woman's apartment and photographing her while she slept," Will added.

"I know... I thought I loved her. I thought I loved all the women I photographed," the man stated with conviction. "But I would never have hurt them. It was a sickness. But I swear, I'm cured."

Valerie looked at Alan Kendrick. He was the definition of someone who could feel insecure about themselves. Someone who wanted to be big. Someone who wanted to be known. Someone who would do the most sordid thing in the world just to be famous.

But the question wasn't whether he *could* be all those things. The question was: *Was* he those things?

Valerie wanted to believe. She desperately desired to have caught the killer. But a growing doubt clouded her mind.

Over on a small table she could see some books. They were on psychology. Some of the textbooks she recognized. And alongside them, she could see a schedule. Alan Kendrick was studying at a college.

"You want to be a psychologist?" Valerie asked.

"Yeah," Alan replied. "I want to help treat people with delusional mental health issues."

"To try to stop someone else ending up in prison like you?" Will offered.

"Exactly," Alan said. "I swear, I'm a reformed man. And I couldn't have killed those women. I read about the most recent victim. Terrible what happened, but I was away on a class trip to the Culver Institute the night she was murdered."

"Can anyone verify that?" inquired Charlie.

"Yes!" Alan said excitedly. "Plenty of people. I was on the trip with seven other classmates and a lecturer. And we stayed there overnight observing nocturnal behaviors of psychopaths while incarcerated. I'll be all over the security footage."

Valerie had no doubt about that. Ever since Arthur Harlow had escaped from the Culver Institute, its security protocols had been completely overhauled, including upgrading their surveillance equipment.

Will turned to Valerie. "I don't think he fits the profile. He's motivated for self-improvement. Our killer—"

"Doesn't want to improve," Valerie stated. "He thinks he's already the finished article and wants to punish the world for not valuing him."

"Exactly, Valerie. I think this is a dead end."

Valerie looked at Alan Kendrick. She felt a guilt bubbling away inside. Where she had seen failure and hopelessness, Alan had shown a desire to reform and help.

I'm being too rash, she thought. *I need to slow down and think this through.*

"We'll need to verify your alibi," Valerie said. "But if what you say is true, then I'm sorry we bothered you."

Alan smiled. "No need to apologize. I just hope you catch him. Of course I'll give you the names of my classmates and lecturer."

"Thank you, Mr. Kendrick." Valerie walked out of the apartment after Alan Kendrick had given her the details they needed to check his alibi.

They walked along the dingy apartment hallway. A neighbor was poking their head out of a doorway.

"He's not the Bone Ripper, is he?" the man said.

"No," Valerie said. "He's innocent. It was a false alarm. We thought he was someone else."

"Oh, that's a relief," the man said, going back inside.

"He must have heard me shouting at the door," Valerie noted. "I'm sorry, guys. I got too carried away. And if his alibi checks out, an innocent man could have had his name dragged through the mud."

"Don't worry about it, Val," said Charlie.

"That's okay, Valerie," Will said reassuringly. "We all make mistakes."

The three walked out of the building in silence. Another dead end. And little did they know the Bone Ripper was at the very same moment plotting his next brutal kill.

CHAPTER TWENTY ONE

Cutting through old magazine and newspapers, the man slowly glued letters to the sheet of paper. As always, he was wearing a mask and wearing gloves to stop the police from finding his DNA.

He had been gratified with how frightened the public seemed after his first Bone Ripper letter had been published in the *Washington Chronicle*.

But he wanted more. He wanted to make the public fear walking the streets.

The letter he was working on would do that, and more.

The man had felt a burning desire to kill more than one woman at a time for some while. But he wouldn't give in to the impulse. He knew about escalation. He knew his blood lust was increasing. But he would remain methodical. He would remain clever.

He would not be caught before he was as famous as Jack the Ripper or Ted Bundy. That was a promise he had made to himself.

Placing the last letter onto the page, he sighed; it was finally ready. He ran a hair dryer across it at full heat to dry the glue, and once finished, he put it in a large brown envelope.

On the envelope itself, he used some small alphabet stencils dipped in ink to write the address without using his own handwriting. He also knew printing the label could have been traced to his printer. His stencil idea was just another stroke of genius; at least that was what he told himself.

"Yes, I am a genius. And they'll know me. They'll be terrified to speak my name," he whispered over the letter.

He was smiling to himself. He'd left some cryptic clues in this letter about his next victim. But would they pick up on them?

It was a dangerous game, but there was method to his madness. Once all this was over, once he had either been caught or escaped into the night, people would pore over those letters like they had with the Zodiac Killer before him.

They would try to decode them. And that would add to his infamy, to his legend.

Posting the letter now was the only problem. He had been using a variety of disguises to stalk and kill. And he'd used another to post the first letter to the newspaper. But he was starting to feel it was an unnecessary risk.

He would find a different way to deliver the letter, and, as luck would have it, his own apartment complex had given him just such an opportunity.

A man on the floor below named Jerry O'Reilly. He was an annoying twenty-something who always got on the man's nerves with his pristine gelled hair and his trendy clothes. He was athletic and handsome. He was always noticed—always.

How the man hated people like Jerry. It all came so easily to them, especially with women.

But Jerry would prove useful.

The man left his apartment and took the elevator down to the lobby.

He would wait. But he had been watching for days. You could set your clock by Jerry.

The elevator went back up and then came down again to the lobby at 8:30 a.m. The handsome, surfer-looking figure of Jerry O'Reilly came out of the elevator into the lobby. With him was his bicycle.

"Hello, Jerry," the man said, concealing the envelope inside his jacket.

"Oh, hey, dude. How are things?"

You don't even remember my name, do you? Well, people will remember me and my deeds long after you're a spec of cremated dust at the end of your insignificant life.

"I'm fine, thanks." The man smiled.

"What's with the leather gloves?" Jerry asked, pointing to the black leather gloves on the man's hands.

"I have a skin allergy that flares up every now and then," the man lied. "I keep these on when that happens."

"Sorry to hear that, dude."

"Off to work?" The man pointed to the bike and the satchel on the rack at the back.

"Yeah, man. Another day of traffic hopping," Jerry remarked.

"That satchel must carry a lot of mail."

"Yeah, it can," Jerry answered.

"You deliver all over the city?" the man asked.

"All over," said Jerry. "I gotta be going though."

"No worries," the man said, smiling at Jerry as he left the lobby and started to cycle outside on the sun-kissed street.

"Idiot," the man said to himself.

He reentered the elevator and headed back up to his apartment, grinning to himself all the way. He smiled for two reasons. The first was that he was sure the letter would have the desired effect and make the public panic and squirm even more.

The second reason he was smiling was that, unbeknownst to Jerry O'Reilly, courier extraordinaire, the man had slipped the letter addressed to the *Washington Chronicle* into his courier satchel.

He was quite confident Jerry would panic and think it was an overdue letter from the day before that had gotten lost in his bag.

The letter would be making its way to the *Chronicle* shortly.

Now it was time for a coffee, and to think about how he would outdo his previous murder. *The more violent, the better. That will catch some headlines.*

CHAPTER TWENTY TWO

Valerie walked into her office at the Criminal Psychopathy Unit in Quantico, surprised to see Icho the *Washington Chronicle* reporter sitting sipping coffee at Valerie's desk. He was playing with an envelope in his left hand, moving it around the top of the table deep in thought.

"That's my seat," Valerie said to the journalist.

"I know," replied Icho. Valerie could smell the cigarettes off of him, and by his even more than usual disheveled hair, it looked like he'd been up all night smoking them.

"I'd offer you coffee, but it looks like you've helped yourself."

"How's the case going?" Icho said, sipping from one of Valerie's coffee cups.

"Why do I get the feeling you want more than a friendly chat, Icho?" Valerie poured herself a cup from the drip machine.

"Okay, I'll dispense with the pleasantries," Icho said. "The *Chronicle* is running a new story this evening. I'll bet you want to know what's in it before it prints."

Valerie felt aggravated. Yes, she did. She never liked dealing with reporters, especially those from the city. They always wanted something in return, and, as an FBI agent, she was duty bound to keep most of her secrets within her department. That made negotiation difficult.

But she had made a deal to at least give him something, if he kept her informed of anything he'd stumbled across.

"What's in that?" Valerie asked, pointing to the envelope in Icho's hand.

"Now, that's the sixty-four-thousand-dollar question, isn't it?" He grinned again. This time, the nicotine stains were even more apparent on his teeth. But Valerie couldn't quite avoid his charm. Icho was unconventionally handsome, and he had that rugged, investigative reporter sleeping in a ditch to get the story kind of look to him.

She thought he'd probably clean up not too bad, but then that wasn't his style. He was all raincoats and grubby shirts with a tie always at an askew angle. There was a strange sincerity to that, though, and he reminded Valerie of reruns of detective shows from the '70s. That and his clear lineage and good looks made him cocky when it came to being persuasive.

But he had met his match here. Valerie would make sure of that.

"If the *Chronicle* is running another story," said Valerie, "then I can assume you've received another letter from the Bone Ripper. Now, you know I could get that taken from you in a heartbeat, don't you? It's just one call. One warrant."

"I do," Icho said. "But I reckon you want this budding relationship to stay open, given that I might get info you Feds can't get your hands on."

Valerie knew he was right. And that irked her almost as much as the smell of smoke oozing out of the man all over her office chair.

"Well, then, let's barter," Valerie said. "I can give you some info for your next article. Off the record, so to speak. But you can put down an unnamed source involved in the investigation."

Icho clapped his hands together with glee. "Now you're talking."

"Okay, we're currently building a profile to anticipate the man's next move. We expect him to be somewhere in his late twenties to mid-thirties. We also think he's someone who feels completely underappreciated by the world. This will be combined with a narcissistic personality where he thinks he should be famous. He thinks the world missed out on recognizing how brilliant he is. If your readers want to help, they can call this number."

Valerie handed over a card with the call desk for her department.

She continued. "We're adding staff to take calls. We're wanting the public to identify anyone they think has a serious persecution complex and has ever shown violent or inappropriate tendencies towards women. Is that enough?"

"Yeah, it'll do for now," Icho said, standing up. He passed the envelope over to Valerie. "I'll make sure that info goes out with the late edition. Thanks, Agent Law."

Valerie felt the envelope in her hand. She wondered just how bad it would be. How much of a panic the Bone Ripper was looking to cause.

Icho walked to the door of the room and looked across at another door that led into the department's main office. "I bet you've got a great evidence board in there," Icho said. "I'd love to see it."

"Don't push your luck, Icho," retorted Valerie.

Icho smiled and left, and Valerie quickly followed, taking the envelope out to the forensics lab.

*

Valerie, Will, and Charlie stood looking at the letter on the touchscreen at HQ. To Valerie, the killer was intent on stoking panic in the city and beyond.

The forensics lab had sent over a digital scan while they carried out critical analysis of any physical evidence. Valerie knew there wouldn't be any. No DNA, no hair, no fingerprints—the killer was too careful. He wasn't about to get caught by being so careless, not yet at least. Not before the blood lust had truly taken over.

The letter itself was a threat. And, unlike other letters sent by other serial killers, this was a specific one. It was a threat to an individual. The Bone Ripper stated in the letter that he knew who his next victim was. He didn't know her name, but he had seen her, and that was enough for him to bring down his knife once more on innocent skin.

Tantalizingly, he mentioned in the letter that the women was engaged.

"I have an idea why he's mentioned the engagement," Charlie offered, staring at the large screen.

"I'd love to hear it," said Valerie.

"You both spoke before about that 'oppositional theory' you had for his motive. That he'd want to punish the good, or at the very least, snuff out life at its best. Well, there you have it. What's more life affirming than getting married other than having a kid? He's targeting an engaged woman. Does an engaged woman represent everything he can't have? The woman who gives herself to one person and not him?"

"Very insightful," Will said, moving his glasses by the rim. "I think, as you have alluded to, Charlie, that the killer has unwittingly told us something new about himself. His main motivation may be recognition, but it is connected to his relationship with women."

Valerie thought for a moment. She closed her eyes and tried to see things from the killer's perspective. A dangerous game she hated to play. It made her feel dirty inside, but it often produced insight.

"Yes," she said after a long pause. "He wants recognition from the public, but he doesn't realize fully that he's killing these women because *they* represent every time he has been rejected. It's really about the women he's killing... He seeks their approval more than anything else. And he knows he can't have it. They won't look at him. They won't love him. So he'll kill women, and he'll gain satisfaction from that. He'll also gain notoriety and attention from the public."

"Two birds with one stone," Charlie mused.

Will stood for a moment, staring intently.

"Hold on," he said. "Could you bring up the two letters side by side, Valerie? I'm terrible with this sort of technology."

"Sure thing," Valerie said. With a couple of taps of her fingers, the scans of the two letters were now on the large screen side by side.

Will hummed slightly under his breath.

Getting to know him over the last couple of months had been a real pleasure for Valerie. But she couldn't help but pick up some of his tells. Some of his own behaviors that telegraphed his thoughts. Humming slightly under his breath was one of them. He had seen something important.

Will let out a gasp. "Ah!" he said loudly. "Look here."

He pointed to the word *kill* in the first letter and then slaughter in the other. Then he pointed to some other words: *butcher*, *murder*, *slay*, *destroy*, *ripper*, *bone*, and a number of others.

"What do you see, Doc?" Charlie asked.

"The purpose of these letters is to frighten, is it not?" Will asked his colleagues.

"Yes, in part," Valerie answered.

"But..." Will seemed excited by a discovery. "While he wants to whip the public up into a fervent terror, he also wants to remain undetected, at least for now. That's why he's used these cuttings from magazines and newspapers."

"He's hiding his handwriting," Valerie noted.

"And any printer that he might have used," added Charlie.

"But he isn't as clever as he thinks!" Will reached up and pointed at the words again. "All of these are violent words. They are about actions, murderous ones. He was a little excited each time he placed the first letter of each of them. Look."

Valerie was astonished. She looked closely. Will was right. Each first letter was very slightly higher than the others on the line. It was almost unnoticeable unless pointed out.

"My God, they're also slightly skewed," Valerie observed. And they were. Leaning at an angle, again almost undetectable.

"What does this mean?" Charlie prodded.

"We have a distinguishing feature now of the man," Will answered, pride in his voice. "He would have placed these letters onto the glue with either a gloved hand or using tweezers."

"And the angle," Valerie continued Will's train of thought. "He would have used his dominant hand."

"Exactly!" Will said, his voice rising. "That's the hand he would have done most of the killing and cutting with. Each time he placed the first letter of a word like *kill* or *murder*, he was becoming aroused. He was excited by those violent words. And that caused him to raise those letters imperceptibly higher than the others with the very hand he would have stabbed with. And the angle…"

"He's left=handed!" Valerie said with grin. "Remind me to buy you a drink when this is done, Will. Brilliant work."

"Why, thank you."

Charlie rushed over to his desk. "I'll run another search for convicted stalkers who've been released. See how many of them are left-handed."

"Great," Valerie replied. She turned and looked at the evidence board, filled with photographs from the murder scenes, maps of the areas, and other info connected to the case.

Valerie always liked to have physical copies of everything up there. The touchscreen was great, but sometimes something would jump out at her when it was all permanently displayed.

"I better print off the new letter," she said, "and put it on the evidence board."

She turned back to the touchscreen and hit print. A printer sprang to life at the rear of the room. That was when she noticed another file attached to the digital version of the letter. She tapped it.

The screen brought up a scan of the envelope in which it had been delivered.

"This is interesting," she said out loud. "There's no stamp on the letter."

"How did it get delivered then?" Charlie said, not looking up from his computer.

"It must have been hand delivered," Will said.

"Not necessarily, Will," Valerie explained. "It could have been delivered by a courier. Either way, this didn't go through the normal mail system."

Valerie felt her pulse quicken. *He's making mistakes,* she thought.

But that would mean his killing was becoming more unhinged. More mistakes might be good for the investigation. But Valerie knew it could only mean more death, even worse than before, was on the way.

"Any luck, Charlie?" she asked.

"Nothing has come up yet," he said. "No one left-handed with a previous stalking record in the area."

"I think we should pay the *Washington Chronicle* a visit," Valerie said. "Let's see if we can dig a little deeper on who delivered that letter."

CHAPTER TWENTY THREE

Valerie took a breath as she entered the *Washington Chronicle* building. It was almost a way to cleanse her mind. She was close to a breakthrough. She could almost taste it.

"We should find out who handled that letter," Charlie said as the two agents walked through the large front doors of the building on M Street.

"Agreed," Valerie said. She walked over to the reception desk.

Behind it was a young woman barely out of her teens. She wore bright red lipstick and had her hair tied back in a way to try to make her look older than her years.

"Can I help you?" she asked, in a voice that suggested she had just stepped out of an Apple Store. Her inexperience was obvious.

Valerie couldn't help feel sorry for her. She remembered what it was like to be that young and hope that she could blend in with more seasoned professionals.

"Hi," she said, showing her badge. "We're federal agents. We understand you received a letter this morning from—"

"The Bone Ripper!" the girl said excitedly. "Yes. I couldn't believe it when I heard."

"Was it you who received it?" Valerie asked.

"Yes," the girl replied. "But I'm not sure how much help I can be. I didn't open it or anything, I swear. I'd get fired for that. One of my friends in the offices upstairs told me what was in it."

The girl's face grew red with embarrassment.

"But please don't say anything. I wouldn't want them to get into trouble."

"We're not going to get your friend in trouble," Charlie said. "Can you remember who delivered the letter?"

"Oh, I couldn't forget. He was a courier." The girl leaned forward and whispered to Valerie. "He was gorgeous."

"Do you know his name?" Valerie asked.

"No," the girl responded. "I'm too shy to ask."

Valerie was disappointed. This was going to take a little more time than she had hoped.

"We'll need access to your security footage." Charlie pointed to a security camera above the reception desk.

"Oh." The girl seemed nervous. "I don't know about that. I think you'd have to ask someone else about it."

"Is there a security guard on duty?" Valerie didn't want to waste time going through official channels. She hoped she could go straight to the source.

"Albert?" the girl said. "Sure. Though he's not much of a guard. He's barely older than me and spends all of his time listening to podcasts when he should be keeping an eye on things. He's probably back down that corridor in the staff room right now. He's on his fifth break today."

Valerie thanked the girl and walked down the corridor with Charlie. They stopped outside the staff room door.

"Polite or not polite?" Charlie asked Valerie.

"Somewhere in between. We need to be quick."

Charlie nodded and opened the door without knocking.

Inside, a man in a security guard's uniform had his feet up on a small table and was sitting reading a copy of *Playboy*.

"Hi, Albert," Charlie said with a grin. He sat down next to him. "I'm Agent Carlson, this is Agent Law. We're FBI agents, and it's your lucky day. You get to help us with an investigation."

"Have… Have I done something wrong?" Albert said, nervously, his big brown eyes glancing around the room as if looking for his boss.

"Nope," said Charlie. "But you've got an opportunity to do something very right. Can you give us a printout of a courier who arrived here this morning from the security footage?"

"Oh… I'd have to ask my boss," Albert said. "But he's off today, can… can you come back tomorrow?"

"No, we can't," said Valerie.

There was a silence.

"What… What happens if I don't help you?"

Valerie felt sorry for the kid. But they had to have that footage today, not tomorrow. She knew nothing would happen, but a white lie was necessary.

"We might have to take you in for questioning," Valerie said. "Maybe you're in on the scheme. Are you in on the scheme?"

Albert stood up. He was smaller than Valerie and she wondered how he'd ever gotten the job.

"I'm not in on any scheme," he said. "And... And... I... I won't be pushed around by the government! My dad says you're always putting pressure on the little guy." He sounded unconvincing. But he needed a little push in the right direction.

"The girl at reception said you'd help us," Charlie said, his voice less jovial and becoming increasingly stern.

"Barbara?" Albert's eyes lit up. Valerie saw the flushed look on his face. The quickening pulse. The release of dopamine. She knew Albert had a thing for Barbara immediately.

"Yes," Valerie said. "Barbara. And she seemed very excited about the case we're on. If you help us, maybe we could let her know you have some information about it. Something you could always tell her over a coffee?"

"You think?" Albert said, hopefully. "Oh, I don't know."

"It's either coffee with Barbara or some more time with us. Which sounds most appealing?" Valerie asked.

"Well," Albert said, "when you put it like that."

*

Valerie walked through the open-plan offices of the *Washington Chronicle*. She could hear the scuttling sound of journalists typing their copy from their cubicles, beneath the unpleasant fluorescent lights.

The place smelled of coffee, cigarettes, and mounting deadlines.

She didn't envy them, but she had to admit there was a romance to being a writer of any kind. Once long ago, she'd even thought about it herself. She'd started writing about her experiences with her mother's breakdown, but it became too painful. Those pages were lost now, either thrown away or sitting at the bottom of a cardboard box in a closet somewhere.

Valerie was on her way to the editor's office. She had some thoughts about how the paper could help her in her pursuit of the Bone Ripper. Charlie, in the meantime, had been sent with a printout of the courier's face from the security cameras to chase that lead.

As Valerie wandered between the cubicles, she spied a familiar face. Or rather, a familiar back of the head.

Icho was typing furiously from his cubicle, alternately sipping coffee and glancing at his watch repeatedly. A blue pen was lodged between his right ear and head.

He was every bit the reporter cliche. But Valerie kind of enjoyed that. After all, she sometimes felt as an FBI agent that she was a walking cliche, too.

Cliches are there for a reason, she thought. *Because they're true.*

Valerie stepped into the cubicle and saw, with horror, that Icho wasn't working on a newspaper piece. Instead, he had a notebook with the words Bone Ripper Book written on it. On his computer screen were lashings of words, all relating to the case.

"Working on something on your break?" Valerie said.

Icho nearly jumped out of his skin.

"Jesus, don't do that!" he said, turning around. "You almost gave me a heart attack."

"Does Williams know you're writing a book on his time?" Valerie asked, raising an eyebrow.

"Keep your voice down," Icho whispered. "I'm just jotting down a few ideas."

"Ideas?" Valerie said, peering over his shoulder. "It looks like you're beyond ideas. It looks like you're a few chapters in. I hope our little arrangement isn't in there."

Icho looked nervously at Valerie. "I do have you in there as a source, but an anonymous one."

"Icho," Valerie said, sighing. "This goes way beyond our agreement."

"I think there's a great true crime book in this, following the investigation," he said. "I could cut you in if I find a publisher?"

"No thanks," Valerie said. "Just keep my name out of it. If I find anything in there that points to me as a source, I will not be happy."

"Don't worry, you have my word as a journalist."

Valerie wasn't sure if that meant a lot or not these days. But Icho seemed like a man out of time. While only in his thirties, he was like a reporter from decades previous, and she felt that his word probably did mean more than chasing a byline.

"What's your angle for the book, might I ask?"

"I'm not sure yet. I'm thinking of how closely some of it lines up with the Zodiac Killer. Especially these letters. How did you get on with the letter?" Icho asked.

"Good," Valerie said. "We might have some new leads from it. At least about the killer."

"Care to share?" Icho asked, grinning.

"I'll think about it if you bring me anything new."

"Only thing I'd say is I had a glance at the reader's mailbag today.

They're loving the Bone Ripper stuff. Can't get enough. A lot of scared and entertained people out there."

"I'm not sure the victims' families would be entertained, Icho." Valerie hated the idea of people making entertainment out of the case. But where there was profit, there would always be profiteers.

"We're not so different, you and me," Icho said quietly. "I don't like the sensationalist stuff either."

"Then don't write it," Valerie said starkly.

"I have to pay my bills," Icho said, with a hint of self-recrimination. "But this book. I swear, if it ever gets published, it'll be a serious piece exploring the terrible impact of serial killers like the Bone Ripper."

But that's just what he wants, Icho. He wants to be written about. He wants the adulation, Valerie thought.

"Okay," she said. "I need to speak with Williams about something. Keep me informed of anything you hear on the street."

"Will do, Agent Law." Icho turned back to his desk and continued typing furiously, staring at his watch momentarily before continuing on again.

Valerie realized he was counting the seconds until his break had ended.

She continued on down the rows of cubicles and then stopped at the editor's door.

"Excuse me, Mr. Williams is busy," a middle-aged woman said, jumping up from her desk as Valerie knocked on the door.

"He'll see me," Valerie said.

"I'm busy!" Williams's gruff voiced shouted from inside.

"It's Agent Law."

There was some sort of clatter inside of something being moved about, before Williams finally loudly said: "Come in!"

Valerie opened the door and saw Williams sitting at his desk. His best attempts couldn't hide the smell of booze in the room. Valerie knew a drinking problem when she smelled one. He was probably boozing comfortably on the leather couch before Valerie came knocking.

"Ah, Agent Law," he said, clearing his throat. "What can I do you for?"

"I need a favor," Valerie asked.

"A favor?" the editor repeated. "Now this is a turn up for the books. I take it it's because of the letter I let Icho hand over to you?"

"It's not about the first or second letter," Valerie said. "It's about the third or fourth."

"What do you mean?" he asked, rubbing the stubble on his chin.

"Don't publish them."

Williams let out a laugh. "That's the best joke I've heard in years. You should take up comedy, Agent Law."

"I'm serious," Valerie said. "The killer wants recognition. He wants to be famous. We should rob him of that. If no one pays attention to his insane rants, he'll grow frustrated."

"Isn't a frustrated killer dangerous?" Williams asked.

"Yes," Valerie said. "But also more reckless. He'll make a mistake trying to compensate for the slight."

"So, let me get this straight," Williams said. "You want me to not only stop publishing the letters, but risk aggravating the man? And then someone at our offices becomes a target? No thanks."

"You're adding to his infamy," Valerie explained. "It's making things worse."

"Agent Law," Williams said rubbing the space between his eyes, "even if I refused to publish these letters, another paper would print them."

"We'd speak with all local publications."

"And I can promise you," Williams continued, "the owners of this paper would get rid of me for killing a cash cow and bring in another editor willing to milk the Bone Ripper for all he's worth. Believe me, Agent Law. I'm your best bet to do this in a reserved way; other editors will make me look like Mother Teresa."

"All you care about is how many papers you can sell," Valerie said. "Death isn't a product you can profit from."

"And that, Agent Law, shows how little you know about the world."

Valerie turned to leave.

"Look, Agent Law," Williams said, his voice a little more subdued. "If it's worth anything. I hope you catch this SOB."

Valerie opened the door back into the writers' pool. The sound of keyboards tapping away came back to her like a tsunami.

All those words, typed in blood, she thought. *I hope Charlie is having better luck.*

111

CHAPTER TWENTY FOUR

Charlie looked at the sea of bicycles chained up outside the run-down storefront. Back in the day he used to cycle a lot. Not recently though. It seemed like the job of hunting serial killers had eroded most of his free time. At least, that's what his wife always told him.

Deep down, he knew this to be true.

Outside, two couriers wearing shorts and T-shirts were having a smoke by the door. Charlie could hear their conversation as he approached. He could also smell the thick stench of cannabis.

"The guy came at me," one of the couriers said, mid-flow through a story. "And I was like, pow-pow-pow." The man shadow boxed on the street as he said this, imitating a flurry of punches against an invisible attacker.

"And that was it?" the other courier said, this one with blond hair and a scar on his left cheek.

"Hell no!" The first courier continued to act out the fight. "I gave him an uppercut. Pow! And then he hit me in the ribs. But I do MMA, bro, my front is like steel. He looks surprised the hit didn't put me down. So I grab him and threw him to the ground. Then I had to choke him out."

"And all that over you cutting in front of him on the lane?"

"Yeah. People are crazy, man."

By this point, Charlie was just a few feet away from the two couriers.

"Hey, guys," he said. "Do you two work at this place?"

"If you mean Mac's, then yeah," the courier with blond hair said. He looked Charlie up and down. "But if you're looking for help, he's not going to oblige."

"Oh, and why's that?"

"Because he hates the cops. And you have cop written all over you."

"How about the Feds?" Charlie said, pulling out his badge.

The blond-haired courier took a large drag on his joint. "Okay, then. He hates Feds, too."

"So, you think he won't speak with me?" Charlie asked.

"I know he won't."

"And what about you two guys? Will you speak with me?"

"Hey, man," the shadow-boxing courier said. "We're not going to get into anything like that."

"And what if I make you?" Charlie stared the shadow boxer down.

"You can't. We're not breaking the law. And I'm not helping a cop, Fed, or whatever."

"What about what you're smoking?" Charlie pointed to the joint in the man's hand.

"Weed is legal in DC, my friend. Recreational and medicinal." The man took a large draw of the joint and blew it in Charlie's face.

"That's true," Charlie said with a smile. "But you know, that would be all well and good if I was a cop. But I'm a Fed. And even though it's legal in Washington, it's still a Federal offense to be caught with it. That means, as a federal agent, I can arrest you."

Charlie put his hands into his jacket and pulled out a set of cuffs.

"Whoa," the shadow boxer said with his hands up, putting the joint on the ground and stubbing it out with his foot. "I didn't know, man. I'm sorry." His defiant demeanor had completely changed.

"I'll cut you a deal," Charlie offered. "I'll turn a blind eye to the weed, but you answer some questions. Deal?"

"Sure." The courier nodded.

Charlie pulled out the picture of the courier from the *Washington Chronicle* security feed.

"Do you know this guy? It looks like his bag has Mac's Courier's logo on it, though it's blurred."

"Yeah," the man replied. "I know him. His name's Jerry O'Reilly. Nice guy. What's he done?"

"Nothing that I know of," Charlie replied. "But he delivered a letter and we want to trace where it came from. Do you know where he lives?"

"Yeah. I do."

Charlie took the details and felt he was one step closer to finding out who sent the letter.

*

Charlie stood on the sidewalk of 14th Street outside a looming apartment building. He stood there with a paper in his hand, making it look like he was waiting for a bus at a nearby stop. Boredom had long since come. But that wouldn't last for much longer.

But he was not waiting for a bus. He was waiting for Jerry O'Reilly.

He was listening to two elderly ladies gossiping about an absent son who never called when Charlie spotted him.

There he was, Jerry O'Reilly, the man who had delivered the Bone Ripper's letter straight to the *Washington Chronicle*.

Jerry was cycling down 14th Street until he stopped outside the apartment building. Charlie walked, newspaper folded under his arm, across the street.

"Hey, Jerry," he said before the courier had time to enter his apartment building.

"Eh, yes, dude? Can I help you?"

"Yes, you can help me," Charlie said. He pulled out his FBI badge.

But then Jerry did something Charlie didn't expect. Jerry started running. He dropped his bike and headed along the sidewalk running as if his life depended on it.

"Stop, FBI!" Charlie yelled. But he wasn't willing to draw his firearm. Not yet, at least.

Charlie chased Jerry along the sidewalk, weaving between the people walking home after a hard day's work.

"Jerry! Stop! I just want to talk!"

Chasing a runner was usually easily in Charlie's wheelhouse. He was ex-military, and always kept himself fit for his cases at the FBI.

But Jerry was fit too. The man rode bikes all day for a living. Charlie knew the courier wasn't going to gas out any time soon.

He was struggling to keep up. Jerry was managing to put distance between himself and Charlie. If he moved away much further, he'd be well out of reach.

Charlie had to think fast. He ran past a small cafe with some seats outside. A young couple was having coffee. Charlie grabbed one of the cups as he passed, poured it out, and then launched it through the air.

The cup caught Jerry square on the back and the shock of it made him lose his balance. He tripped up over an uneven piece of sidewalk.

Charlie apologized to the couple, dropped a few dollars onto their table, and then ran to where Jerry was on the ground. He was getting to his feet just as Charlie reached him. Charlie grabbed his arms, put them up behind his back, and cuffed him.

"You shouldn't have run away, Jerry. Are you okay?" Charlie said, panting.

"I didn't do it!" Jerry said. "I swear."

"We'll find out soon enough." Charlie led Jerry back along the road toward the apartment building.

"How was I supposed to know?" Jerry asked, being marched along the sidewalk.

"Know what?"

"That there was weed in the package. I just picked it up like any other. I only found out when the guy I delivered it to tore it open in front of me."

Charlie was puzzled.

"So, you think I arrested you for delivering cannabis to someone as a courier?"

"Wait? If it's not that, what is it?" Jerry seemed genuinely bewildered.

Charlie stopped and turned Jerry around. He uncuffed him. Then he turned him around again and looked him in the eyes.

"Jerry," he said, "I'm here because of the letter you delivered to the *Washington Chronicle* earlier. The one with no stamp."

"Oh, thank God," Jerry said. "I'm so sorry I ran, dude. I was sure I was getting involved in something over my head."

"Well," Charlie continued, "don't thank the heavens too quickly. That letter was from the Bone Ripper."

Jerry's face drained of color. "You don't think I'm the Ripper do you? That dude is a monster. I read about him in Icho's column."

The two men were now standing outside the apartment building. "If you can tell me who gave you that letter, Jerry, then I can cross you off my list of suspects." How Charlie wished there was a list of suspects, but Jerry didn't need to know that.

"But that's the thing, Officer."

"Agent Carlson, Jerry."

"I don't know who sent it, Agent Carlson."

"Well, that's not going to look good for you, Jerry."

Jerry started panicking again, breathing faster and shifting around nervously.

"Don't try to run again. This time I'll hit you with something much worse than a coffee cup." Charlie moved his coat to the side and showed his holstered revolver.

"Oh, man," Jerry said at the sight of the gun, wiping sweat from his forehead. "Look, I found that letter in my courier satchel this morning.

I thought it was a piece of mail I'd missed from the previous day. I thought it was weird there was no stamp on it."

"And was it?"

"No," Jerry said. "I delivered it first thing because I thought it was so late. Then I asked Mac about it back at the courier station, and he told me there was no record of it. It hadn't been scanned or anything."

"So, it just magically appeared in your satchel?"

"Dude, I've been thinking about it all day. Someone must have sneaked it into my satchel without me knowing."

"And who would do that?"

"I don't know," Jerry said. "But it could have been anyone. I'm out all day, and someone could have slipped it in at any point. Most of the time I have it closed, but when it's empty, I sometimes don't lock it up."

"Where do you keep your biked at night?"

"In my apartment. But I live alone."

"Okay, Jerry," Charlie said. "Don't go far. Here's my card if you think of anyone who might have done that."

"Yes, Agent, I will. I promise."

"On you go," Charlie said, picking up Jerry's bike and handing it to him.

Charlie watched Jerry disappear into the lobby of the apartment building. He looked up at the countless windows on the building, a sea of eyes glaring back.

For a moment, he considered that the killer could be someone from the apartment. That could be a line of inquiry

Valerie was waiting back at the *Chronicle* for him. He'd pick her up and run his findings past her. Whether they lived in the apartment or not, whoever slipped that letter into Jerry's bag was the killer.

CHAPTER TWENTY FIVE

The man looked out of the window down at the street and couldn't believe his eyes. Jerry O'Reilly was being questioned by the law.

Am I caught? he thought. *No, Jerry doesn't know anything.*

The man's best guess was that they had traced the letter back to Jerry as a courier. But since Jerry didn't know who had slipped the letter into his satchel, there was no way he could incriminate him as the Bone Ripper.

But he was still angry. Angry that he had slipped up so much. He thought using Jerry as a courier wouldn't come back to him, but there he was down on the street.

Then, something interesting happened. Jerry walked back into the building on his own, and the cop or Fed arresting him walked across the street and went into his own car.

Is that it? Is that as close as they'll come?

If Jerry had been able to ID the man as the maker of the letter, then surely the officer wouldn't have driven away. He would have called for backup or entered the building to make an arrest.

The man thought for a moment. Maybe he had gotten away with it. But things would need to move faster. If he wanted to be known, if he wanted to kill as many victims as possible, he couldn't afford to wait any longer. The FBI might put it together.

I'll kill tonight then.

He moved quickly, putting his wallet on the table and taking off a ring that he wore on his index finger.

Nothing to identify me.

The man grabbed a jacket and some cash and left the apartment.

Moving down the hallway, he was stopped momentarily by old Mrs. Goldstein.

"Off out, are we?" she said with a kind smile.

I'd love to slit your throat, he thought, but instead kept the pretense of his calm exterior. "Yes, just going to grab some milk."

"Oh, sonny, I could give you some."

Interfering old bag. I wish I could snap your neck. "No, no, I appreciate that. But I need a little air anyway, I have a headache.

"Poor thing," Mrs. Goldstein said and patted the man on the cheek. "If you want a cup of coffee or anything, you come by when you want."

I'll come by, all right. Like a plague in the night. The last thing you'll ever see is my grinning face. "Absolutely, Mrs. Goldstein. Lovely to see you. Thanks. Have a great evening."

The man turned and moved to the elevator fast enough that Mrs. Goldstein couldn't delay him anymore. He still liked the idea of killing her. Maybe his last victim. But he hoped he had more time.

Once out of the apartment, the man headed two streets away to a small piece of waste ground that was surrounded by a dilapidated fence. He slipped through the fence and through a dense line of bushes. In the bushes, he uncovered a metal tool with a T-shaped end.

He then moved out of the bushes and finally stopped at an old rusted manhole cover. He placed the tool into the cover and leveraged the cover off. Obscured from prying eyes by the fence and bushes, he descended, pulling the manhole cover back into place above him.

In his pocket was a small flashlight. He pressed the rubber button and it dimly lit his way. He climbed down about twenty feet. The ladder was wet and rusted, but still sturdy.

Placing his feet on the ground, he felt the thin layer of water that had seeped in from the manhole cover above during a recent downpour. He moved his flashlight left and then right.

This was an old sewer system that had been part of a factory many decades previous. The factory had stood derelict for years before finally being pulled down. But the unused sewers underneath were still to be decommissioned. The man new this wasn't likely to happen any time soon. Not with how much it would cost the district.

He moved along a tunnel, ducking his head down low in several places, and in others being able to stand tall. Finally after several twists and turns, he found what he liked to call his "HQ."

A few days earlier, he'd moved anything incriminating down there, just in case someone searched his apartment. The fact that Jerry O'Reilly had been questioned made it clear that this was the correct decision.

They'd never know to come down here, he thought as he sat in a small alcove next to a black backpack. Inside, he pulled out a lantern. When he turned that on, he was lit with a brilliant beam, but it had nowhere to escape down there. It only lit the darkness below.

The man pulled out a mirror and carefully applied the makeup. He'd watched a makeup artist use latex and foundation to completely change the shape of a person's face.

He used spirit glue to attach the latex pieces, before adding a fake beard with spirit glue. Staring back at him from the mirror was a different man. It wasn't himself anymore. To him, the bearded man staring back was just one more face of the Bone Ripper.

"They'll know me," he said out loud. His voice echoed along unseen tunnels and passageways deep beneath Washington, DC.

The president has secret bunkers and labyrinths beneath the White House, why not me? That thought made him chuckle. Yes, he was special. He was as important as any president or leader. And he'd make them know it.

He put his hand into the backpack and found a knife and small hatchet. This was his only dangerous move. It was dangerous to carry weapons if he happened to be searched. But he couldn't do what he intended with his bare hands. At least, he didn't think he could.

The last thing was to take a pair of gloves he would put on before reaching his target. He stuffed them into his right pocket.

The man headed along one of corridors, his feet echoing as they slapped against the thin veneer of stagnant water. He then reached out and put his hands on another metal ladder. This one was a little more eroded, with some of the struts broken. But with a little effort, he could skip those. He grabbed hold of the cold metal and then headed upward. This time, he appeared in a small derelict building. One that sat within the factory grounds but had yet to be demolished.

He emerged from it, and within moments was walking along the streets of Washington, now a good distance from his apartment. He hopped onto a bus and sat. No one there paid any attention to him, but he saw a woman reading the *Washington Chronicle*. The latest story by Icho, their investigative reporter.

The woman reading had a fearful, curious, enthralled look on her face.

This pleased the man. She wouldn't have paid him any attention as a lover. No. But that pretty lady would pay attention to his legend. To his deeds. He felt the knife under his coat against his skin.

He smiled and waited for his stop. A stop that would take him to his next kill.

CHAPTER TWENTY SIX

Valerie had been silent for most of the drive back to Quantico. She was thinking about the case. Keeping her eyes on the road as Charlie drove, she had hoped that their search for the courier would have given them something more substantial. Instead, it was another uncertain turn in a case of uncertainties.

"You're sure Jerry O'Reilly isn't involved?" Valerie finally said.

"The guy was clueless about it, Val," Charlie said. "I believe him. Someone slipped that letter into his satchel."

"We need to run some database checks on everyone working with him," Valerie said. "The other couriers, the managers. Everyone."

Charlie took their exit on the highway. The car rumbled slightly.

"Man, I need to get that fixed," he said. "There's a weird clunking noise every now and then."

"We're all a little road weary, Charlie."

Charlie laughed. "Ain't that the truth."

"We should run a search on the apartment building as well," Valerie said. "Just in case we get lucky. It could have been a neighbor who slipped it into his satchel."

"Possibly." Charlie now sounded as gruff as the car. He cleared his throat. "But Jerry O'Reilly stated that he keeps the bike in his apartment and he lives with no one. I'm not sure how a neighbor would get the opportunity."

"Passing by in the building," she said. "Maybe they dropped it in while talking to him. Or perhaps he left his bike for a moment and had to rush back to into his apartment to get something he forgot. There would have been opportunities."

"True," said Charlie. "But this killer doesn't feel like and opportunist, does he?"

Valerie thought back to Tanya Brenning. Her legs cut off while she was tied up. Charlie was right. The killer wasn't an opportunist. He was thinking things through. He was planning.

"I don't know," Valerie said. "Perhaps he waited for a moment he knew he'd encounter Jerry with his bike."

"Yeah," said Charlie. "But that would have been a mistake. He's either made an error, if that's true, or it's not someone in the apartment building. It's someone else."

"We'll run checks on all of Jerry O'Reilly's close contacts. You never know."

There was then a silence between them. It had weight. It was the silence of disappointment. The silence of knowing a killer was still free to roam, when it was their duty to stop him.

As if feeling it himself, Charlie flicked on the radio. "I think we need to decompress a little."

He flicked through some radio stations. Charlie didn't know, but one of those brief stations was playing a song that cut into Valerie's mind like a knife. Charlie didn't linger on it for too long before switching to another station. But it was long enough for Valerie to identify it.

It was long enough for the song to bring forward a terrible memory.

Valerie's mind played the memory like an old VHS tape. Warped. Fuzzy. But rendering an unmistakable image. It was the image of her playing with her sister when Valerie was about six years old.

Suzie was toddling around, still in diapers. But she could say a few words, and she doted on Valerie. The feeling was mutual.

Valerie was drawing on a piece of paper. She remembered that much. She was sitting on the floor, scribbling with coloring pencils.

Suzie came over and watched intently.

Somewhere in the house, their mother was puttering around. She had an old FM radio on. And that very same song Charlie had momentarily paused on while flicking through stations in the car.

As I walk along, I wonder what went wrong...

Del Shannon sang the song, an old one from the fifties, his voice floating through Valerie's mom's radio.

Suzie clapped gleefully as Valerie drew a big house with a smiling family standing outside of it.

"You, me, and Mom," Valerie said, pointing to the happy figures on the paper.

Suzie loved this. She took the picture and went to show their mom. But she only got as far as the door.

I'm walking in the rain, tears are fallin' and I feel the pain... the song continued. The words mixing with what happened, and with what it meant, like colored paint running together.

Little Valerie looked up from her place on the floor to see her mom appear through the doorway. Suzie handed the picture to their mom.

At first, their mom smiled. But then something happened. Valerie remembered a slight facial tick that would happen when her mom was about to detach from reality. She saw something in the picture.

"Who are these people?" she said quietly at first. Then louder. She rushed over to Valerie. "Who are these people!?"

"It's us, Mom," Valerie said. But she already felt a cloud brewing.

"This isn't us," her mom said. "These are the Other People."

Even at that tender age, Valerie knew about the Other People. Her mom would occasionally spiral. Her moods would change, and then she would start talking as if the people in their family photos were somehow *not them.*

The Other People became a part of Valerie's mom's delusions. A shadowy group of people who looked like the family and wanted to replace them.

And I wonder where she will stay, my little runaway... Those words circled in Valerie's mind. She remembered. She remembered her mom taking a pair of scissors and cutting out the family's smiling faces. She then put them down the garbage disposal.

And just like that, she flipped again.

"A lovely picture, Suzie," she said. "Thank you."

For weeks, that picture was given pride of place on their refrigerator in the kitchen. The picture of the house. The picture of the family. The family with missing smiles.

Valerie snapped back into her awareness.

Charlie was entering the underground parking bay after passing security at the Mesmer Building.

Just as the car dipped down into the dim lights of the parking lot, Valerie's phone rang. "Run, Baby, Run" played once more as it always did. The caller ID said it was Tom, Valerie's boyfriend.

"I've got to get this, Charlie. I'll meet you up there." Valerie got out of the car and stood near the entrance where there was still cell phone signal.

"Hey," she said, answering.

"Am I missing something, Val?" Tom asked.

Then Valerie remembered. She had planned to go for a bite to eat with him that night. Another promised evening. Another one foiled by her commitment to her duty. Sometimes Valerie wished she just didn't care. That she was just going through the motions in her job. Then she could have more of a normal life.

But no, that just wasn't her.

"I'm so sorry, Tom," she said. "I didn't expect us to get back this late to Quantico."

"I'll call the restaurant," Tom said glumly. "Looks like it's just reruns of *Friends* for company tonight."

"I'll make it up to you."

"Where have I heard that before."

"It's a tough case," she said.

"It always is, Val. But I guess you wouldn't be you if you didn't keep chasing until the end." Tom's voice softened. "I'll take a rain check."

"I do miss you, Tom," Valerie said. Her voice wavered.

"Are you okay, Val?" he asked, sounding concerned.

Valerie wanted to blurt it out in one shout. But the pain of her childhood, of her relationships with her sister and mother, it was too deep, too complex to rid herself of in one rant.

Tom wanted to build a life with Valerie. *But what if I'm like them?* she thought. *What if I'm ill, too? I can't put him through that.*

"Val?"

"Yeah. I'm okay, Tom. Just tired."

"Why don't you tell me what's on your mind?"

"Jesus, Tom, you sound like my old therapist. It's not that easy."

There was a silence.

"You don't need to take it out on me, Val," he said. "I'm just trying to support you."

"I know. But—"

"Don't push me away," Tom continued. "Your job taking you off for days at a time I can handle, but you shutting me out, that's when we have problems."

I've shut out everyone. I can shut out you, too, Tom. I can shut out the world.

Charlie suddenly appeared from a stairwell to the side of the entrance.

"Val!" his voice echoed through the parking bay. "He's killed again!"

CHAPTER TWENTY SEVEN

Valerie was unnerved as the news filtered through. As she and Charlie walked underneath the bright yellow police tape, the cordoned off trailer looked like a holiday resort gone bad. Countless rows of trailer homes bathed in the worrying blue and red lights from three patrol cars blocking access to vehicles.

"Two victims, Charlie?" Valerie said as they walked up a small hill through the trailer park to the scene of the crime.

"He's escalating," Charlie replied.

Beneath the darkening skies, rows of oak trees swayed in the wind, delineating the streets of the park. Once, long ago, those trees had been part of a huge forest south of Washington, but the space had been shaped by developers to create Jefferson Place, an upmarket trailer park for those rich enough to own a holiday home there.

"There's Will," Valerie said.

They had informed Will as soon as they heard. And there he was, already on the scene, standing outside the large white mobile home that looked bigger than Valerie's entire apartment.

"Hello," he said as the FBI agents approached. "This is different."

"How do they know it was the Bone Ripper?" Valerie asked.

"I already asked one of the attending police officers, but he was too in shock to answer."

Valerie walked up a set of small wooden steps into the trailer. It looked pristine. At first, there was no obvious sign of any bodies, but that all changed when she walked into the master bedroom.

On the bed were a young couple, no older than twenty-five. They were lying on their sides and were embracing each other.

Valerie could feel her breathing stagger slightly at the sight. The bed was saturated in blood.

"What in the name of God happened here?" Will said. To Valerie, it sounded as though he wanted to leave.

"You okay, Will?" Charlie asked.

"I've never seen anything like this," he said, staring at the two dead bodies embracing each other in the bed, their mouths partially open, congealed blood upon their lips.

Valerie put on some forensics gloves and leaned over the bodies. She could smell the horrid stench of blood, oxidizing in the air. It had saturated the bed sheets into a crimson stain several feet wide.

"He didn't tie them together," Valerie said. "There are no marks on the wrists. He must have gotten them to lie here like this by threatening them. Maybe even telling them they'd be okay."

Will and Charlie looked on.

"He's cut off the ring finger of the man's left hand," Valerie continued. "And from the woman's too. By the way the blood spilled out from the fingers, their hearts were still beating. So, I'm assuming they were alive and conscious."

"Did he take the fingers as a souvenir?" asked Charlie.

Valerie looked closely at the faces of the couple. They were staring at each other, their eyes glassy and vacant. But there was something about the way the man's jaw was sitting that was awkward.

Putting her hand into her pocket, Valerie retrieved a small pocket flashlight. She shone it into the barely open mouth of the man. The beam caught something shiny. The glint of metal was wrapped around something pale and white and long.

Valerie's stomach lurched. She looked in the woman's mouth. She saw the pale white thing, but no glint of precious silver.

Standing back, Valerie took a breath.

"He cut off the woman's finger because she was wearing her engagement ring on it," Valerie speculated. "The killer then placed the finger, still wearing the ring into the man's mouth. The killer then cut off the man's finger and put it inside the woman's mouth. He then slit both their throats and carved Bone Ripper into their necks."

"How do you know they were alive when they had the fingers placed in their mouths?" Will asked.

"Teeth marks, Val?" Charlie asked, his voice quiet and somber

"Yes," she said. "When he cut their throats, they bit down in pain, leaving an impression on the skin of the fingers."

"This is an abomination," Will said. "The killer wanted to punish both of them for being happy."

"It's recognition again." Charlie looked around the room. "The female victim was engaged, and he could never have something like that. He wants that type of recognition. So instead, he'll get it with blood and terror."

Will looked mournfully at the engaged couple. "The first question

125

in my mind is, why two? And why now?"

"There must be a reason for it," Charlie mused. "The killer is always so meticulous in his planning. There must be a motivation behind why he killed the man as well. Up until now, it's always been women on their own."

"Yes," Will agreed. "This changes his MO."

"Unless…" Valerie was looking at something.

"What is it, Valerie?" asked Will.

Valerie moved over to a small coffee table. Sitting on it was one coffee from Starbucks, and next to them a brown paper bag.

"There is one coffee here," Valerie explained. "And it's full."

"One of the victims never got a chance to drink it, guess."

Valerie opened the brown paper bag. Inside there was a wrapped sandwich.

Walking back to the side of the bed, she looked down at the dead couple. She felt sick for them. Ready to start a life. And this evil piece of work had taken it from them in the most horrendous way.

"I think this was a crime of opportunity," Valerie said. "The single coffee and sandwich, still wrapped. Imagine the killer follows the woman to this trailer. He enters when she's alone. He then marches her into the bedroom. While he's about to begin his handiwork, the fiancé arrives back at the trailer.

"It's a coincidence," she continued. "The male victim didn't expect his partner home. He came in to eat lunch by himself. The killer reacts and improvises in the cruelest of ways."

"If your theory is correct, that means this isn't a change in MO," Will expanded. "The killer will still target women by themselves after this."

"Yeah," said Valerie. "But you can be sure Williams will print a story about how even couples aren't safe together, creating more panic."

"Our prime concern, then," suggested Will, "is to find out how he knew this woman. He said he knew his target in the last letter."

"But that doesn't mean he personally knew her, Will," Charlie elaborated. "Maybe he knew what she looked like. He'd been following her. Stalking her. Maybe he encountered her one day randomly and saw she had an engagement ring, and she fit his purpose."

"Except he didn't know her!" Valerie said, rushing past her two colleagues to the wall opposite. "Look!" Valerie was pointing to a pretty wooden frame that sat on the wall below some other

126

photographs.

"Charlie, Will. I know how he's choosing his victims! We've got to go, now!"

CHAPTER TWENTY EIGHT

Williams's office at the *Washington Chronicle* was colder in the dead of night. Valerie could feel a draft of air coming from somewhere, and it brought with it a subtle chill, one that could only exist while the rest of the world slept.

She looked at her watch. It was nearly 3 a.m.

Charlie and Will paced impatiently, but Valerie remained calm. At least on the outside.

As they waited for Williams and Icho to arrive, Charlie looked out at the city.

"It's peaceful from up here," he said. "All those lights. You wouldn't know there's a killer on the loose."

"Are you getting all philosophical these days, Charlie?" Valerie said, smiling. She sat down in one of Williams's large leather armchairs away from his desk. She rubbed her eyes.

Will and Charlie looked at each other, both with concern on their faces.

"I wish you'd rest more, Valerie," Will said. "Your job isn't worth your health."

"I'm fine," she said. "I wish you would both stop fussing."

"That's what partners do," Charlie said.

"Indeed," Will agreed, dipping his head slightly and looking over the rims of his glasses with an affectionate smile.

Valerie was glad to have both of them in her life. Charlie had been a trusted partner and friend for some time. But the way Will looked at her. It was with paternal care.

She wished she'd had that as a kid. Maybe she wouldn't be so messed up inside. Maybe Suzie wouldn't have ended up in a psychiatric ward. Maybe her mother would have had someone to lean on when she needed it. That was a lot of maybes, and they had never panned out for Valerie.

Her father had worked away often. And by the time Valerie was eight, he'd left to be with another woman. It was a chicken and an egg situation. Which came first? Her mother's instability, or the wreckage that lay about her, creating a fractured mind?

Will turned to look at Williams's bookcase.

"He has Epictetus's musings," Will observed. "There's no way he's read them I would have thought. Must be for show."

"Epictetus?" Valerie asked.

"An ancient Greek philosopher. A Stoic, in fact. He believed we should only contend with the things we can control. Events outside of our control, no matter how painful or horrifying, should simply be accepted, freeing us from worry."

"I don't know about that," Valerie said, sighing. "I think there's always the chance that you can change things. I'd rather go down fighting."

"Perhaps that's why you're in pain, Valerie, my dear," Will said.

Before Valerie could react to that comment, the doors to the office opened. In walked Williams in a suit and Icho behind him, as disheveled as Chicago is windy.

"Where the hell do you get off summoning me here at this ungodly hour?" Williams said, brushing past the investigators and grabbing a bottle of scotch from the nearby mantelpiece. He poured himself a drink and sat down angrily behind his desk.

"I was awake anyway," Icho grumbled, slumping down in one of the armchairs.

"You writer types," Charlie said. "Always burning the midnight oil."

"For peanuts, it seems." Icho rested his head against his hand.

Valerie stood up.

"We were just at another Bone Ripper crime scene," Valerie stated plainly.

Icho sat up. He fumbled for his notepad and pen from his inside pocket. "Go on…"

"Two victims this time," Valerie explained. "A young couple, engaged to be married."

"So the sick bastard went through with his threat to kill an engaged woman?" Williams said, taking a slug of scotch. "Icho, make sure you get all this. I want it going out in today's edition."

"On the wall of their bedroom was this." Valerie pulled out her phone and showed it to Williams. "It's a framed announcement. The couple had previously announced their engagement with an ad in a paper. Then they framed it, hung it on their wall, and dreamed of their future."

"Yeah, so it's an ad, and?" Williams grumbled.

"Notice anything about it?" Valerie pushed. She pinched in on the image. "Look closely, just above the bottom frame. The tops of two words."

"*Washington Chronicle*," Williams said quietly.

"It seems your paper is now actively involved in the case," Charlie said.

"So, they put out an ad?" Williams poured some more whiskey. "Why does that mean I have to get out of bed and come over here to work? A place I can barely escape during the day."

Valerie put her phone away and returned to the armchair, crossing her legs.

"Mr. Williams," she said. "Why did the killer choose the *Washington Chronicle* to send his letters?"

"We're a big paper."

"True," she said. "But I'll let you in on a little secret. Sending to one newspaper doesn't fit his profile."

"If I may," Will interjected, "we have enough info on the killer to build a partial profile. We believe he is mainly motivated by wanting to be seen. He wants fame."

"Don't we all," Williams quipped.

"But," said Charlie, "he is motivated by rejection. He wants to world to know who he is. He wants to rewrite his life's story by gaining the fame and power over women that he's never been able to have in his real life. He does that by being as sadistic as possible. As calculated as possible. So, then: If he wants to be seen, why did he send his letters *only* to the Chronicle and not any other outlets or national news stations?"

"Maybe he's a fan of our work," Williams said, half-joking.

"Not quite a fan," Valerie said. "But he has a connection to the paper, and I believe it's his way of saying thanks. You see, I think he's picking his victims from the very pages that you print. That ad for our recent murdered couple. But what about the others? Can you search their names in your records?"

"Hold on a minute," Williams said. "I'm not sure I like the sound of the paper I run being held responsible for giving this sicko ideas."

Icho cleared his throat.

"Let's not be hasty, Boss," said Icho. "Agent Law could get a warrant and gain access to our database. And besides, I think this is a pretty fascinating angle. The relationship between the media and violent killers. It's a great angle for a few articles." He lowered his voice. "Or a book."

"All right," Williams sighed. "Give me the names."

Valerie passed a piece of paper with the names of the Bone Ripper's first three victims.

It only took a minute or so for Williams to have done three searches via the computer on his desk. Each time, a hit had been produced. Williams looked very worried.

"It seems you were right," he said, his voice as dejected as his posture. He turned the screen around for everyone to see.

Valerie rushed over and looked at the display.

"An article mentioned the killer's first victim, Cassandra Miller, for having a DUI and getting into an altercation with a local bar owner," Valerie summarized "Then, Shelly Bridges was quoted in an article a couple of years ago about the positive effect hiking had had on her mental health."

"What about Tanya Brenning?" inquired Charlie.

"Her name was mentioned when she won a Business Commerce award."

Will stepped forward to look at the screen. "So we have a crime report, an article, an award listing, and finally the engagement announcement for tonight's victims. All different sections of the paper, and all different types of article. A pity. If there was a pattern there, it might have helped us anticipate his next target."

"But the connection is there," Valerie said. "We could put out an announcement alerting people that if their name has appeared in the *Washington Chronicle* over the last few years, they should be vigilant."

"Don't you dare!" Williams said angrily. "You do that and no one will ever want to appear in our paper ever again. You might as well burn down these offices with that sort of talk, Agent Law."

Valerie wondered if it was indeed a little hasty. But it was all she could think of in the moment. She just wanted the public to take the danger seriously. It was more than a simple story in a newspaper or an item on the local news channels. The killer was real. The lives he had taken were real. The pain he was imprinting on the world was real, too.

"If you put that out, you might as well fire every employee in this building," Williams continued. "Do you want them to have their livelihoods on their minds?"

"Employees…" Valerie said quietly to herself.

Icho leaned forward in his seat. Valerie saw him write something down and then stare at her. It was as if he were trying to communicate something.

He's thinking what I'm thinking. What if it's not a reader who's killing these people? What if it's someone who works at this paper?

"We need to think of the public first," Charlie replied to Williams. "You can't put your paper ahead of the people."

"Quite right," Will agreed. "We *should* at least warn people that..."

"Never mind," Valerie said. "I think I have everything I need here. Thanks for coming in so late, Williams."

Williams eyed Valerie with suspicion, seeming surprised that she'd so quickly dropped the idea. The truth was, Valerie had a much more important one now in her mind. And the last thing she wanted to do was alert the editor of the *Chronicle* to its existence.

"Good night," Valerie said, leaving the office.

"What was that about?" Will said, walking beside her.

"I thought you'd push more," Charlie said.

"No, what if—"

Icho came running out of his boss's office, now revitalized He rushed up to Valerie.

"You don't really think someone who works here is the Bone Ripper, do you?" he asked quietly.

"Now *that's* a great idea," Charlie said spontaneously.

"No comment, Icho," Valerie said. "I don't know where your loyalties lie."

"With the truth," he said with conviction.

Valerie was impressed. She was beginning to think he really cared about facts rather than sensationalism. But she couldn't trust him completely. He was, after all, an employee of the paper.

All Valerie knew was that, in the pit of her stomach, she felt someone connected to the paper was behind the killings. It was time to find out how good her instincts really were.

CHAPTER TWENTY NINE

Charlie kept his eyes on the road, but it was Valerie, his partner, who was on his mind. He drove through the nocturnal streets of Washington DC, the lights reflecting off of a thin veneer of water on the empty streets. Sometimes they pooled like vast holes into a mirrored world where everything you knew was upside down and inside out.

Valerie seemed different than usual to Charlie. He had been watching her the last few days. There was something bubbling underneath in her voice. Something finding its way up through her tangled nerves.

She was on edge, and more so than he'd ever known her. And he knew it wasn't just the case. It was her family. But she'd never let him in all the way. Charlie knew that visits to her sister were weighing her down, but she wouldn't open up about it. Not in the way that a close friend and partner should have.

She was keeping her pain to herself.

To Charlie, that made him question if Valerie really trusted him. Because trust is born out of sharing burdensome secrets. He'd shared a good few of his own with her throughout the years. But he was beginning to realize that sharing was a one-way street.

"It's a fascinating idea, you know?" Will said from the backseat as the wheels of the car splashed through countless puddles. "That someone working at the *Chronicle* is the killer."

"Or at least helping him pick victims," Valerie thought out loud.

"There'll be hell to pay if we pull the *Chronicle*'s name through the mud, Val," Charlie pointed out.

"Why is that?" Will asked.

"Because," Valerie said, looking at Will in the wing mirror, "there's an unspoken rule that government agencies shouldn't interfere with press institutions. It makes people nervous. They start to think we're looking to control media, which is what some other countries do."

"Dictatorships," Charlie said. And Charlie knew a thing or two about totalitarian regimes and dictators. He thought for a moment about his tours in Iraq and Afghanistan. The soldiers he'd fought alongside. Good, bad, indifferent. The many wounded. The many who never came home.

Yeah, he knew what could happen if a government tried to control a people's ability to express themselves through the printed word.

"Ah," Will said. "Understandable."

"So we'll have to tread carefully," Valerie said. "We don't want to implicate anyone at the *Chronicle* until we have something concrete. Jackson will have a heart attack if we leaked the fact that someone working there might be the killer or in cahoots with him."

Valerie's phoned buzzed.

"Who's texting you at this time of night?" Charlie asked, hoping there wasn't something wrong with her sister.

"It's Icho," she said. "He's letting us know about a man named Duncan Reece. He worked at the paper." Valerie took in a sharp gasp of air. "No way. He was a section editor at the paper but was let go for harassing a female member of staff, sending her abusive messages on social media and even turning up at her apartment drunk on several occasions. She filed a restraining order against him and he lost his job. Icho is worried it's him."

Charlie's mind raced. *Is this it? Do we have our man?* Charlie yearned to put him in cuffs, to stop the killing. And then be home with his wife and family.

"How long ago was this?" he asked.

"I don't know, hold on." Valerie sent a reply to Icho. "I've asked him."

Almost immediately, her phoned buzzed again.

"Well?" asked Will.

"You guys won't believe this," Valerie said with astonishment in her voice. "He was fired just two weeks before the first victim was murdered."

"We could have our trigger point," Will said. "He could have been feeling out his stalking tendencies, then when he was fired, he unraveled and started killing."

"Exactly my thought," Valerie agreed. "That might have sent him over the edge."

But Charlie was unsure. "He can't have unraveled that much, the killings have been meticulously planned. They aren't the actions of someone losing control."

"We'll find out soon enough," Valerie said, looking at her phone. "I have his address, let's go."

*

Charlie had driven as fast as he could. They didn't want the suspect to get away. Not when Valerie was so certain he was now escalating his kills. Even a few lost hours was enough for him to claim more victims, and Charlie knew this.

They had to be fast.

Charlie mounted the curb and pulled on the handbrake after the car came to a stop. He drew his gun.

"Let's move."

"Will..." Valerie said.

"Don't worry, I know the drill," Will replied. "I'll stay back here."

Charlie rushed out of the car, keeping low on the street.

"That's his apartment building there," Valerie said, moving over to the door of the towering building.

Valerie pushed the services button.

"Hello?" a gruff voice answered.

Valerie pulled out her badge and showed it to a security camera above the speaker. "This is the FBI. We're investigating a murder. Open up."

The door buzzed, and they were in.

"He's on the third floor," Valerie said, moving to the stairwell as the elevator was out.

Typical, Charlie thought as they ascended. He didn't want to be too breathless by the time they got to the third floor, so he moved at a slower speed.

They reached the floor and headed out of the stairwell across a brightly lit red carpet and along a stretch of hallway.

Valerie pointed to the perp's door.

Charlie nodded. He could feel the adrenaline pumping. His army training had taught him, however, to never sit in that feeling. Adrenaline was good for survival, it could make you stronger, faster, temporarily, but it could also put you so on edge that you made a mistake.

He slowed his breathing and then turned, slamming his fist on the door.

"Duncan Reece! FBI! Open up!"

But there was no answer. There was, however, a sound, like two

135

people in conversation.

They waited, and Charlie knocked on the door again. Shouting the same warning.

The sound of conversation inside continued, and now it was rising into an argument. Someone started yelling, but the words were muffled.

"He's not coming out if he's in there," Charlie whispered.

Valerie's face looked drawn. "What if he's out already, killing again?"

And that was when they heard it: a scream came from inside the apartment.

Charlie felt a reactive surge of adrenaline. He had to intervene. Now he had probable cause to enter.

He turned and put his shoulder against the door. It buckled under the force, the lock splintering the wood of the door frame.

"FBI!" Charlie shouted. "Don't move."

But the apartment was quiet, all but for the television that had been left on. A cat sat on the floor watching it, two people in an old film arguing over something inconsequential. That was all they had heard.

Charlie and Valerie scanned the rooms. They were empty. The suspect was gone.

In the bedroom, there were empty bottles of beer scattered on the floor.

"He's drinking," Valerie said. "Just like Dahmer and some other serial killers did. Maybe he has blackouts."

But that didn't sit well with Charlie.

"The killer doesn't come across like the type who is drunk or on something when he kills," he said. "He's too together."

"Maybe," Valerie said. "But he's the only suspect we have. We've got to find him."

Charlie thought for a second. "I know it's a long shot, but what about the woman who took out the restraining order against him at the *Chronicle*?"

"Great idea," Valerie agreed. "I'll contact Icho and get her address. We've got to be quick. He could be there already for all we know."

*

"Will," Charlie said, turning to his colleague at the rear.

"I know," Will said from the back seat. "I'll stay here."

This time, Charlie had parked slowly outside of the woman's home.

136

It was a semi-detached house not too far from the *Washington Chronicle* building.

"We'll need to go in quietly," Valerie said. "If he's here, we don't want to scare him off."

Valerie moved to get out of the car, but Charlie held out his hand.

"Val," he said, looking at the layout of the street. "If he sees us both coming, he'll go, and this place is like a maze. Could you let me scout it out first? If I go out there like I've just driven home from working late, he might not run off."

"I don't like you being alone, Charlie," Valerie said.

Charlie was always grateful for Valerie's loyalty.

"I know," Charlie said. "Give me three minutes, and then follow?"

Valerie sighed. "Okay."

Charlie exited the car. A breeze fluttered along the street catching the trees that lined the sidewalks. It was a leafy place. There were hedgerows, bushes, fences, and a lane that ran between the houses. Plenty of places to hide.

It was a labyrinth. And if the suspect was even half familiar with the area, he could lose Charlie quickly.

Charlie pulled at his tie and yawned walking down the street. He looked at his phone and pretended to answer it.

"Yeah, I'm just coming. Sorry... I know... If you'd just let me speak... I had to work late, Honey, there was no..." He pretended his wife had hung up on him. "Great," he said, loud enough for the suspect to hear, but not so loud that it sounded performative.

Charlie was selling himself as a resident of the street. He just hoped it worked.

He walked past the address they were looking for and entered the yard next to it.

He glanced momentarily at the woman's yard next door, but a glance was all he needed. A glint of light from the streetlights nearby illuminated something in the corner of the woman's yard. Two pinpricks of light.

Someone was hiding in the darkness.

Charlie pretended not to notice and disappeared to the rear of the next house. As soon as he was out of view, he rushed silently over a fence at the rear of the property, then circled around so that he ended back on the street without the shadowy figure knowing.

Moving in front of the woman's house, he nodded to Valerie in the car and then pointed to the yard.

Valerie nodded back, drew her gun, and then stepped out onto the street.

It seemed that was enough to finally provoke a response from the shadowy figure. It stood up out of the shadows, revealing a pale, tall man, and he moved toward the rear of the property.

If he's running, we'll lose him back there, Charlie thought. And so he was left with no choice.

He rushed after the man into the darkness.

The man saw him coming and leaped over a fence. Charlie followed.

"FBI! Stop or I'll shoot!" Charlie yelled.

The man rushed around a corner, and Charlie was close on his heels. Then, from the shadows next to some rubbish bins, Charlie saw the pale man leap out at him.

Charlie fired once, but the man already had a hold of his hands, pointing the gun to the ground. The bullet ricocheted off the concrete, kicking up debris.

"Charlie! Where are you!" Valerie yelled from somewhere nearby in the darkness.

But Charlie didn't have time to yell. He had to deal with this now. His life depended on it.

The pale man thrust a fist toward Charlie's face, catching him on the cheek. Dazed, Charlie pulled back to try to get distance enough to shoot. But the man was on him, closing in.

He threw another punch. Charlie's instincts kicked in, and he dodged, letting the man's fist thump into the wall behind them. A loud crack of bone and knuckle sounded.

The pale man let out a yelp.

Now was Charlie's chance. He thrust his shoulder into the man's stomach and then pulled up his legs, slamming him to the ground. Then Charlie grabbed his wrist, pulled it into a lock.

"One more move, and I'll break it," Charlie said, looking at the man on the ground with grim determination.

"I wasn't going to hurt her," the pale man said.

"Yeah," Charlie answered, sarcastically. "Of course you weren't."

Valerie now appeared running along the path toward Charlie. She helped put the man in cuffs.

"We've got him, Charlie! I can feel it," Valerie said.

But Charlie knew getting the man back to HQ and putting him under pressure was the only true way to find out.

CHAPTER THIRTY

Valeric glared at the man before them. Underneath the harsh overhead lights of the interview room, he looked even paler than he had on the way there.

Beside him sat a lawyer in a gray suit, this one assigned by the state.

Pulse racing, Valerie knew the interview would be crucial. She felt so close to finally putting the Bone Ripper case to bed.

"So, Mr. Reece," Valerie said from across the metal table, Will and Charlie flanking her. "Do you know this woman?" Valerie showed him a photograph.

The suspect nodded mournfully. "That's Louisa... Louisa Flockhart."

"Isn't it true," Valerie continued, "that you were fired from your job at the *Chronicle* for harassing her? And then a restraining order was put in place?"

"They call it harassment," the man replied. "I call it justice."

"Justice?" Will said, leaning forward. "You have a sense of that?"

"Of course. Right is right," Duncan Reece answered.

"Interesting," Will said, clearly turning to his own thoughts for a moment.

"Can you tell me then, Mr. Reece," Valerie asked, "why were you sitting in her yard in the early hours of this morning?"

"She needs to know!" The man's voice grew angry.

"Needs to know what?" Valerie sensed a revelation. "To know *you*? To make you famous? So the world can value you?"

The man shook his head.

"No," he said. "I don't care about me. But my brother!"

Valerie was sideswiped by that. She didn't see it coming.

"Your brother?" Will asked. "You care for him?"

"I loved him," Reece explained. "He was my little bro. He was happy. Then that woman entered his life and ruined him."

"Help me understand," said Valerie. "Why are you stalking Louisa Flockhart?"

"Because," the man said, agitated, "they had kids together!"

"Hardly a crime," Charlie finally said.

"Maybe not in your courts," Reece said. "Maybe not in this room. But in here." He pointed to his chest. "To anyone with a heart. It was a crime what she did."

"I want to understand, Mr. Reece," Valerie said. "Tell me why she had to pay, and what you were going to do."

"I... I just wanted to scare her," he said. "I just wanted her to feel even a fraction of what I felt. She took the kids. Then she made up vicious claims about him to get custody. He was left with nothing. He threw himself in front of a train two days later. You know what that does to you? To lose you little brother like that?"

Duncan Reece started to cry. "It tears you apart. And there's no justice. Nothing. It's all *his* fault for leaving us, according to Louisa and others. But the truth is, she drove him to it, she drove him to it! I just wanted to scare her..."

Valerie's heart sank. Not just at the story. Whether it was objectively true or not, the man felt aggrieved. But none of this fit the profile.

"Where were you on the thirteenth?" Charlie asked, pointedly.

The man started to laugh.

"What's so funny?" Charlie frowned.

"Look at your own records and see for yourself," he said." I was in jail on the thirteenth. Drunk and disorderly outside a bar. I got hammered and nearly got run over trying to cross a busy street. Cops put me in jail and I sobered up."

"We'll see if that pans out," Valerie said.

"Val," Charlie said quietly. "Can we have a chat?"

Valerie nodded.

The three investigators left the room and then entered the soundproofed observation room next door. As always, Jackson Weller was there peering through the glass. He'd come into work in the middle of the night to see the interview.

"Well?" he asked.

"You look as tired as I feel, Boss," Charlie said. "And I think we're all going to be a little more exhausted... This isn't our guy."

Valerie said nothing. She wanted it to be the killer. She desperately did. But deep down she knew Charlie was right. She felt the man wasn't lying about where he was the night Tanya had been murdered. She walked over to a computer terminal and searched the database.

"Wait," Jackson interjected, his hand up. "You found this guy stalking a woman, and you said he worked at the *Chronicle*?"

"He did in the past," Valerie sighed. "But Charlie is right. This isn't him."

Jackson threw up his hands in frustration and paced for a moment before turning to his three investigators.

"Can someone explain this to me?"

"Jackson," Will said softly. "The man has empathy oozing out of him. He loved his brother. He wants revenge. But he's never grown violent. I can't say he never would, what he's done to the lady by stalking her is awful, but he feels inside he has *moral authority* to do this. The Bone Ripper doesn't need that to placate what he does. He doesn't care about morality."

"He also wasn't carrying any weapons, Jackson," Charlie added. "We searched his car and found nothing, either. And his apartment had nothing suggesting he was plotting to kill. What we have here is a guy who doesn't have it in him to kill, but wants to scare. I think that's about it. We can all agree the Bone Ripper has no qualms about killing."

"And..." Valerie said, looking at the computer screen, "his alibi checks out. He was in jail the night Tanya was killed."

"Besides," Will added, "he was a section editor at the *Chronicle*. That's a prized job. This man is falling apart, but he has been successful. We're looking for someone who can't quite make it to the top and hates the world for it."

Will's words floated through Valerie's mind. *Can't make it to the top...*

"Wait a second," Valerie said, tapping her lips with her index finger as she thought through the idea. "What would agitate the killer's sense of pride more, to never be listened to, or to get close? Close enough to show what he can do, but never be rewarded in the way he thinks he deserves?"

"So, we're not talking about a complete failure then?" Charlie asked in return.

"This would require a shift in our profile," Will added. "But I couldn't rule it out. Take us where this leads, Valerie."

Will's support landed like that of a caring father figure. It was the warmth she needed in a world filled with coldness. She felt a surge of pride. As if she wanted to gain Will's acceptance.

"Acceptance!" Valerie said.

"Acceptance?" Jackson seemed bemused.

"Yes!" Valerie said. "Let's imagine the killer got close to where he wanted to be in life, but no matter how hard he tried, he couldn't quite get to the promised land. With relationships, with friendships, with his career."

Valerie began to pace back and forth, thoughts and insights rushing through her mind. She just had to speak them out to see how formed they truly were.

She went on: "Let's think about it. The killer has some sort of connection with the *Washington Chronicle*. He picks his victims from its pages. He sends his letters to them to publish, and only them. What if it isn't that he just wants to be famous, what if he wants to be *accepted*? But not just by anyone? What if he wants to be accepted by the *Washington Chronicle* itself? A complete acceptance that he hasn't been able to gain in his life. He's come close, so close he could taste it, but he's never been fully invited into the club."

"A freelancer!" Will said excitedly. "That would fit this new profile point."

"Yes!" Valerie said, clenching her fists. "A freelancer would work *with* the Chronicle but not *for* them. He wouldn't be on their salary. He wouldn't have an office or cubicle. He would be just outside of things. Permanent positions would come up, but for some reason, Williams would never hire him full time."

"That would explain," Charlie mused, "why he's only giving the *Chronicle* the scoop. It would also explain why he's picking his victims from there."

"How so?" asked Jackson.

"As far as I see it," Charlie continued, "the people in those pages are the lifeblood of the paper. Without them, there's no story. It's almost like he's choosing people he thinks don't deserve to have attention, when he's languishing unnoticed by those at the *Chronicle*. By the world, even."

"Brilliant insight, Charlie," Will said.

"Come on," Valerie said, hurriedly as she exited the room. "This could be it."

Jackson, Charlie, and Will followed Valerie as she hurried down the hallway to the command room. Inside, the evidence board and the touchscreen stood.

On the touchscreen, Valerie quickly pulled up pieces of reporting from the *Chronicle*, as well as the front pages each time a murder was reported.

Valerie glared at the screen.

"What's on your mind, Valerie?" Will asked.

"An idea," she said, zooming in to the three front pages. "What if the freelancer, looking for the acceptance and adulation of the *Chronicle*, wanted to be on the front page?"

"Well," said Jackson, "that's why he kills, isn't it? He wants to be front page."

"Maybe..." Valerie let out a gasp as she zoomed in further to the front page reporting the murder of Tanya Brenning. "But what if it's more than that? What if he literally wants to be on the front page in a way that he never could?"

Valerie rushed over to her coat, hanging over a chair. She pulled out her phone and dialed.

Her heart pounded in her chest. *Was this it? Have I figured it out?*

"Hello?" a voice said groggily over the phone.

"Icho, this is Agent Law. I'm currently staring at the front page you worked on for the Tanya Brenning case."

Icho coughed and then yawned. "Oh, yeah. What about it?"

"There are three photographs," Valerie explained. "One is of the parking lot your photographer took with you over my shoulder that night. It shows the car with Tanya's body blurred out."

Valerie stepped closer to the touchscreen and leaned in to scrutinize something.

"Icho," she said. "There are two smaller inserts. One shows a still from the security camera that picked up the killer when he kidnapped Tanya. But the second, it's of the field where the car was later dumped, showing the road next to it."

"What about it?"

"Did the same photographer take all three shots?"

"Yeah," Icho said. "Why?"

"Because the shot of the field, it's empty. There's no car or crime scene."

"So?" Icho said. "The county police removed everything in the morning. The photo was taken after that."

"No, Icho," she said. "There are no tire tracks running across the field. That photo was taken *before* the murder."

"It's probably a stock photo the photographer found online somewhere," Icho said. "I'm pretty pissed, though. We paid him for it. He shouldn't pass that off as his own."

"Why would there be a stock photo of a random field with no point of interest, Icho?" Valerie asked. "Besides, it looks almost exactly the same. My bet is, the photographer took this days before."

"Then how would he know there was going to be a murder there?"

There was a silence. The phone line buzzed lightly.

"Oh no," Icho said, his voice the closest to distraught Valerie had ever heard it. "You think the photographer is the Bone Ripper?"

"Let me guess," Valerie said, using the profile she had now just completed in her mind. "He's a freelancer. Very eager to do well. But arrogant. Narcissistic. Acts like he should be the paper's top photographer. Always tried to get on payroll, but bizarrely stopped asking just before the murders started. Does that sound about right?"

"He's a weird guy, Agent Law," Icho said. "But he really pushed to come with me on these cases. And slashed his asking price for his freelance fee. I... I never thought for a second... I'm so sorry."

"You don't have to be sorry, Icho," Valerie said, looking around for and finding a pen. "It's not your fault. It's only a theory at the moment, so I have to ask for your discretion. We need to put finding this guy and talking with him ahead of a scoop."

"Of course," Icho said. "What can I do?"

Valerie believed him. For all his scruffiness, his gruff demeanor and his desire to turn the case into a book, she believed he genuinely wanted the truth to come out to protect the public.

"Can you give me his address?" Valerie asked. She scribbled down the address, but couldn't believe what was staring back at her. "Thanks, Icho. I owe you."

"I hope you get him."

The call ended.

Valerie handed the address to Charlie.

"No way!" Charlie looked frustrated. "I ran a check on everyone in that building, but nothing came up."

"We've got to go back there and catch him. Now," Valerie said gravely.

"Where are we going?" Will asked.

"To the same apartment building where Jerry O'Reilly the courier lives."

CHAPTER THIRTY ONE

Eric Grant stared at the newspaper article in front of him. The paper lay on his kitchen table.

This one will get me the recognition, he thought to himself. *It's going to be a masterpiece of a story.*

The article described Heather Maguire, a twenty-four-year-old woman who had turned her back on a successful career as a model to teach children at a high school

So high and mighty, Eric thought, looking at her photograph. She was beautiful, no doubt, but teaching kids? What was so special about that? Why should she get attention when the Bone Ripper should be the star of every edition, every page?

He felt a surge of arousal as he put the funnel into the top of the bottle, filled it up with clear liquid, and then sealed it off carefully.

Acid will make this one special, he thought, imagining pouring it over the woman's face, melting away her skin down to the bone. And he was going to do it while she was alive. *I'm going to be bigger than Dahmer, bigger than Bundy, bigger than Gacy, bigger than any killer that came before me.*

Now all that was left to do was to put on his disguise, put the bottle in his bag, and go give the public another dreaded kill.

*

Valerie didn't wait for Charlie to be at her back. She saw that Eric Grant's apartment door was thick and heavy. Neither of them were kicking it in. Instead, she drew her gun and squeezed the trigger.

The lock burst open.

"FBI! Eric Grant, you're under arrest for murder!" Valerie yelled, lunging into the apartment.

She instantly smelled it. A chemical smell. Stronger than a cleaning agent. Acid, maybe?

Charlie ran in behind her, brandishing his revolver. Valerie looked along a hallway. It was dim, the sun not yet having risen. She pulled out her flashlight and scanned the place.

The beam of her light touched a wall in a small room off the side.

"My God," she said out loud. "It's like a shrine in here."

And it was. Eric Grant had plastered the wall with every publication he'd been featured in. Then there was a wall with awards. But they were from grade school. Then a swimming certificate. Another certificate saying Eric Grant had completed a photography class at a college.

Valerie then knew what it was. These were not achievements that Eric Grant took pride in. He wanted more out of life. These awards were a reminder of how little he'd achieved in his adult life in comparison to his ambitions.

Exiting the room, Charlie said: "Clear. Another apartment. Another absent owner."

"I think he's on his way to do something terrible," Valerie said.

"Maybe we'll get lucky, Val. Maybe he's sleeping off drink somewhere."

"No, can't you smell that chemical?" Valerie asked.

"Yeah," Charlie replied. "What is it?"

"Look over here." Valerie pointed the beam of her flashlight into the kitchen. On the table there was a closed copy of the *Washington Chronicle*.

"I think," Valerie said, worry etched through her voice, "that he's taken some sort of acid to his next victim. And he's identified them in this edition of the *Chronicle*."

"How can we possibly know who it is?" Charlie sounded tired and dejected. They had been up for hours chasing leads. But they had to push through.

Valerie put on gloves and picked up the paper. She had picked up the skill of speed reading during her studies. It meant she could scan large bodies of text and pick up pieces of important information. It was never as accurate as reading the entire text, but it had served her well when cramming for exams in the past.

She sat down at the table, but the thought that the Bone Ripper had sat in the very chair picking his next victim sent a shiver through her body.

Charlie flicked a light on and kept watch in case the killer returned.

Valerie started scanning the pages of the *Chronicle*, one by one. She ran her finger down the text of each article, noting the headline and then picking out important words and concepts here and there.

Article after article, page after page passed. Until she stopped suddenly. It was an article about a supermodel who had become a teacher.

Valerie thought for a moment. *Yes, you'd like this, wouldn't you, Eric? I know you've been bottling acid in here. I can smell it. And your twisted mind, desire to shock, what better shock than scarring a model who has become a selfless individual? You hate the adulation she's received, don't you? You can't stand others getting credit, getting acceptance.*

But you'll make her pay, won't you? You'll make them all pay for ignoring you.

"This has to be it," Valerie said, picking up her phone and calling Quantico.

One of the admin staff on night shift picked up at the Mesmer Building.

"Maria?" Valerie said. "I need an address. Can you help? Her name is Heather Maguire, she teaches as Oakton High School. As soon as you have it, send it to me, and contact local police to send an emergency car there right away. The Bone Ripper is there. Thanks."

"What now?" Charlie asked.

"Let's join Will back down at the car. It's a waiting game, Charlie. Either we get the address quickly, or Heather Maguire is about to be horribly murdered."

CHAPTER THIRTY TWO

"You're almost asking for this," Eric said, tying the woman's arms to her bed. "I mean, your window frames are so old. I was able to push one open from outside and climb in. And here you are in bed, sleeping for the last time."

It had been so easy for Eric. He knew Heather's address from the photographer who had worked on the story. And the house, in the early morning hours? Simple to find, and simple to enter.

"Please," Heather said. "Please don't hurt me. You're not going to—"

"No," Eric said. "I'm not that kind of a criminal. I'm not interested in *having* you. I just want to make an example of you. Do you know me?"

"No..." the woman said, her voice quivering.

"I'm sure you do," he said. "Do you even read the papers?" He leaned over and put a gag across her mouth. Once it was tied tightly and she couldn't speak, he told her the true horror of her predicament.

Leaning in closely to her face, he said: "I'm the Bone Ripper."

The woman let out a muffled cry. Tears streamed down her cheeks.

Ha, she knows me all right, Eric thought. *And now she knows who I really am, she is aware she's about to die.*

"It gets difficult, you know," Eric said, rummaging around in a bag. "Coming up with more shocking ways to kill people. But I have a public to satisfy. It's a burden of being famous. I suppose in some way you understand, what with having been a model before. Strange that you'd throw away the attention and change careers."

Eric pulled out a clear glass bottle from his bag. "But I think you'll find your death will be the best yet. And when they realized you were alive to experience such a terrible way to go, it'll shift some newspapers, I'll tell you that."

The woman let out a gurgled cry as Eric moved toward where she lay. He took the cap off the bottle.

"I have to be *very* careful with this stuff, Heather," he said. "I won't bore you with the chemical name. All you need to know is that it's acid. And this acid can melt through skin, chewing through muscle and ligament, and then even start dissolving the bone. And just think, you'll feel it all, gushing over your face."

Heather was screaming now, but the gag muffled each scream into a whimper. Eric thought she was trying to say please or stop, but it didn't matter. She was just a thing to him. A thing to help him get recognition.

"Here we go," Eric said, moving the bottle above her face and beginning to tip it.

That's when he heard a car skid to a halt outside.

*

Valerie leaped out of the car onto the quiet street. She saw no patrol vehicle, no police presence at all. They were on their own.

"We're not waiting for backup," she said to Charlie.

"Will?" Charlie said.

"Yes, yes, wait in the car. I know."

Valerie and Charlie moved with one purpose: To save Heather Maguire from the Bone Ripper's brutal actions. They drew their guns and moved as one and with purpose.

But Valerie was terrified they were too late. She thought of the acid eating into Heather Maguire's face. Of it consuming flesh and muscle and bone. It was a horror almost too unbearable to consider.

This thought pushed her on. But could she be certain the killer was nearby? Valerie moved, ducking down to avoid being seen. She stopped by a small wall and peered intently at the house in question.

The windows were obscured by red curtains in some places and half opened blinds in others. The deep red of the curtains was like blood, and the darkness of the interior world appeared to Valerie like portals into some unthinkable abyss, where monsters and their deeds lay in equal measure.

Charlie slumped down behind the same wall.

"It's too exposed," he said.

Valerie knew he was right. Charlie always had an eye for approaches; his military training relied upon those keen insights.

The front of the house was exposed, with little cover. But there was nothing that could be done about that. They couldn't wait any longer.

Was the Bone Ripper in there? Had he already disposed of Heather Maguire?

Valerie couldn't wait any longer. She studied the front of the building momentarily, looking for a sign that she was right.

And there it was: a window that had scrapes along its frame. It had been forced open with a tool of some description. Valerie now hurried toward that window. She pushed it open and the air of the house met her. Every home had its own scent, its own air. This air carried with it danger, and she knew it.

She and Charlie climbed inside. The house was quiet, but it was not serene. Valerie turned to Charlie. "You hear anything?" she whispered.

Charlie paused for a moment.

"Not yet. Come on."

Valerie took point and walked through a doorway into a darkened hall. There were no windows in the hallway, and so the darkness felt like an unnatural opposition to the light outside.

Moving slowly, Valerie stepped forward, but Charlie held placed his hand on her shoulder.

"You hear that?" he asked, his voice a sunken whisper.

Valerie strained… Yes, there was something. A strange sound, indistinct and uncertain. Valerie stepped forward slowly, the floor creaking under the footfall. Another step. Then another.

Each time the sound grew in volume. A buzzing. Or was it a dripping? A generator? Valerie thought.

Reaching a closed doorway, Valerie placed her hand on the handle of the door. She swallowed nervously as she turned it, not knowing what was on the other side.

A neon light met her gaze, bright and unnatural.

A large aquarium sat beneath the sill of a bay window. Its ultraviolet light cast an unearthly glare across a room populated by two large La-Z-Boy chairs and a television.

The aquarium bubbled and buzzed as Valerie's blood pressure did likewise. But their pursuit of the killer remained unfinished.

Turning, Valerie headed back into the hallway and then listened intently as she moved. *Did I… Did I hear something there?*

Creeping along the hall, watching each shadowy corner and doorway, knowing that her life, her partner's life, and Heather Maguire's life relied upon her vigilance and decision making, Valerie strained her ears again.

It was as if a sound was just out of reach, almost entering into her conscious awareness, not enough to be truly heard, but felt. Valerie experienced this like a presence filling the house, and it was not a benign one.

Charlie was behind Valerie, and as if reading her apprehension at *something* happening in the house somewhere in the dimness, he tapped her on the shoulder.

Valerie dropped back slightly and looked at her partner. He looked deep in thought.

"You hear something?" Valerie whispered.

"Yes," came Charlie's reply. Once again, his crystal clear hearing had come into play.

"I think I hear someone groaning, like they're gagged," he said.

That description made Valerie sick to her stomach. For a moment the image of Heather Maguire dying on a floor somewhere in that house, melting away beneath a layer of violent acid, was too much. She batted it away.

Her instincts were important, but her training was there too. She used her skills to steady her nerves.

It's time to move, she thought. She looked at Charlie and pointed to the end of the hallway where a door stood shut, steadfast against their movements.

They rushed together, quiet, uncertain, watching the doorways, the corners, the shadows, and with each step they neared the room where the noises were coming from.

As they approached... Yes, the groan. Valerie heard it, too. It was the sound of a woman gagged, trying to say something, anything.

Valerie thought of the other victims, how they had been gagged. Of Tanya... Poor Tanya, gagged and cut in half.

Shelly.

Cassandra.

The lovers in the trailer, cut down before having lived.

Anger came to Valerie. *No more*, she thought. *No more.*

She moved to the door, and did not hesitate. She opened it and entered slowly, trying to calm the adrenaline.

And there she was; Heather Maguire, tied to her own bed by the hands of the Bone Ripper. She was gagged, but she seemed to be unharmed.

The red curtains of the room fluttered from a breeze of air coming from the only window. It was open, wide enough for a killer to have escaped.

Valerie then smelled it. The same chemical she'd smelled at Eric Grant's apartment. *It's him*, she thought.

151

Charlie carefully untied Heather, who let out a horrid cry when he took the gag off of her, burying her head into his shoulders.

"It's okay," Charlie said. "You're safe now."

"No... No... No..." the woman repeated, her eyes moving erratically.

"You are, it's okay," Valerie offered, gently. "We're with the FBI."

"No... No..."

At first Valerie thought that Heather was having a complete breakdown, but that was when the horror of the situation presented itself. Valerie turned to look at what Heather was gazing at. It was the curtains. The crimson red material moving in the draft from outside. Moving... And momentarily outlining the shape of a large man standing to the side of the window behind it.

"Charlie!" Valerie cried out.

Charlie reacted quickly, but the large figure moved from the curtains, his right fist clenched, catching Charlie in the face with a violent blow.

Charlie staggered, pulling a small nest of tables over onto their sides as he did.

And it all happened in an instant.

Valerie watched in utter terror as the Bone Ripper raised his left hand. There was something in it. The smell of acid stung Valerie's eyes as the attacker thrust the bottle of acid that was in his hands directly at Charlie.

At the same moment, Valerie jolted forward and grabbed one of the knocked over tables. She leaped in front of her partner and held aloft the small table, shielding her partner.

The acid sprayed across the table, scorching its wooden surface. Valerie launched the table at her attacker, and he ducked out of the way. As the table struck the wall, the Bone Ripper leaped out of the open window into the yard at the rear of the house.

Charlie was dazed but untouched by the acid. He reached out and caught Valerie's arm, saying sluggishly: "Don't go after... Val..."

But Valerie saw the distraught Heather Maguire sitting in the corner of the room. She had come so close to being hideously tortured by the Bone Ripper. Valerie saw in her eyes the look of utter trauma.

She remembered feeling that trauma, too. As a child. The fear of your world ending.

Valerie couldn't let the Bone Ripper get away to carry out another despicable attack on another woman somewhere out there.

No.

This stops. Now.

Valerie pulled away from Charlie's hand and moved to the open window. Looking down to the grass outside, she saw it was burning, melting away. The Bone Ripper had dropped the rest of his bottle of acid as he fled.

She carefully stuck her head out the window and saw the shape of a figure disappear around the corner of the house.

"Stop or I'll shoot!" Valerie commanded. She leaped through the open window, avoiding the acid on the ground, and ran, arms outstretched, gun in hand.

She stopped at the corner and darted her head out. Eric Grant was on the move. He was running along the yard and back into the street.

Valerie fired a shot, missing him. The bullet lodged itself in a nearby elm tree.

She moved again. *I will not let you get away.*

Valerie thought about the victims, about the women who had been preyed upon, about the engaged couple who had been butchered, all for fame, all to be accepted.

She didn't pity this man. She hated him.

Valerie moved out into the street, and what she saw chilled her to the bone.

The Bone Ripper, Eric Grant, had pulled Will Cooper out of the back of the car and was now holding a knife to his throat.

"Don't move, Eric. There's nowhere to run."

Charlie now appeared, staggering behind Valerie, still dazed and sluggish, but still backing up his partner. He frowned in concern at the sight of Will as a hostage.

"Dammit," he said under his breath.

Eric and Valerie locked eyes. And a thought crossed Valerie's mind. *Fame, fortune, infamy... He'll do it to be known... No time...*

Valerie closed one eye, squeezed the trigger of her gun, and watched as Eric Grant's head pulsed with blood, before he collapsed to the ground.

Will staggered forward and then dropped to the ground alongside the now dead body of the Bone Ripper.

Charlie and Valerie rushed to their friend.

"It's okay, Will," Valerie said, holding him. "You're okay."

Then the true horror struck. Will started coughing up blood.

Valerie looked at her friend and pulled Will's sweater down. Blood oozed out from a large knife wound in his chest. Eric Grant had already stabbed Will moments before Charlie and Valerie ran out onto the street.

He was losing blood. Valerie felt sick as she and Charlie awaited an ambulance, trying to stem the flow of blood from Will's chest.

EPILOGUE

Valerie sat beside the hospital bed and looked at someone for whom she cared deeply. This time, however, it wasn't her sister, Suzie, highly medicated and delusional. No, this time it was Will Cooper, resting and responding well three days after he had been stabbed.

Will slowly opened his eyes.

"Oh, hello, dear," he said to Valerie. "I didn't know you were here."

"It's the medication, Will," Valerie said. "I hear it feels delightful."

Will laughed and then coughed. "Not exactly delightful, more like tiresome."

Valerie had spoken with Will a couple of times since his operation, and each time he was becoming stronger and more lucid. She was relieved he was getting better, though there would be a period of recovery.

"Has any of this put you off being part of the team?" Valerie asked. It had been on her mind.

"Of course not," Will said. "But maybe in the future I'd be safer with you and Charlie than sitting in the car." He smiled gently. Laughed. Then coughed again.

"Leave the jokes to me," Valerie said.

"Tom not with you?" Will asked.

"He's cooking up a storm back home. He sends his best."

"He's a good man, Tom," Will observed.

"I know," Valerie said. "He's great."

"And you've just caught an infamous serial killer," Will continued. "A little time off on the horizon. Good friends and colleagues."

Valerie wondered where this was going.

"Yeah," was all she could say.

"Why then, Val," Will said, sitting up painfully in bed and fixing his pillows, "are you so unhappy?"

Valerie let out a sigh. "Why do I get the feeling I'm not going to get much past you?"

"I'm not meaning to pry, Valerie," he said. "But I am concerned about you."

Valerie thought that typical of Will. He was the one in the hospital and yet he was thinking about her well-being. A thought fluttered through for a moment. How she wished her own father had been like Will.

"I know you have issues with your past, Valerie," he said. "Your mother, your sister. I know. But until you either confront those issues or express them by confiding in someone, I fear they are going to consume you. And in a dangerous job like yours, you do not want to be preoccupied with pain. Distraction could prove fatal."

Just a week earlier, and Valerie would have rebuffed this line of talk. But having nearly lost Will as a friend and colleague, she now felt him more precious than ever. And that had eroded some of her wall, though not all.

She could never tell him that she was afraid she was losing her mind like her sister and mother. Will would be duty bound to make sure she wasn't in the firing line in her work if he knew. He would go to Jackson.

But Valerie felt she could tell him *something*.

"Will," she said, "my mother wrote a message to me just after the Harlow case. I usually had nothing to do with her. I never visited her, and I never spoke with her. She was dead to me in many ways."

"But something has changed?" Will said, an eyebrow raised.

"The message," Valerie explained. "She gave it to Suzie to pass on to me. But there was something in it. Something that I don't fully understand, but it relates to my past. And I *have* to talk to my mom about it. But the only thing is, she now won't see me. I don't know what to do."

Will seemed deep in thought for a moment.

"Valerie," he said. "If you don't mind me saying, I never hear you mention your father. Is he not around? Could he not help persuade her to see you?"

If Valerie had avoided seeing her own mother for years, she had avoided her father for even longer.

"He left when I was very young," Valerie said. "And... I have a memory of him and my mom fighting. It's not clear. I sometimes have dreams about it. But I think he might have been violent towards her."

"It seems to me," Will suggested, "that your issues aren't just with your sister and mother, but your father, too. Valerie, perhaps there are two reasons to try and contact him."

156

"Oh," Valerie said, knowing Will was right.

"The first is that perhaps he could help with the message you received. Help you understand it. Maybe explain it. The second reason to find him is it will help give you some closure as an adult. It will help you come to terms with your childhood trauma."

"I wouldn't even know where to begin."

Will laughed. "Valerie, you're an esteemed FBI agent. Surely that will help in searching for him?"

The door to the hospital room suddenly opened.

"Is there room for one more?" Charlie said, sticking his head into the room. "Although there's a stern-looking nurse around here that told me it's one visitor per patient at the moment. And I'd hate to get on her bad side."

"Can't you use your charm?" Valerie said, standing up and giving Charlie a hug.

"Nope," he said. "Some people are completely immune to my shimmering personality... How you doing, Will? I brought grapes and that journal from your office you wanted."

"Ah," Will said. "Thanks so much, Charlie."

Charlie put them on a small table beside the bed.

"I heard from Jackson, Val," Charlie said. "He's rubber stamped the report. There won't be anything to answer."

"Answer?" asked Will. "What's this?"

"There was a witness," Charlie said. "They saw Valerie shoot the Bone Ripper. They claimed she didn't ask him to put down the knife."

"I knew I had to react," Valerie said. "He wanted to be infamous. He'd have certainly gotten that killing Will, who he probably thought was an FBI agent or police officer. And if he was killed after that, he'd still be famous for it."

"I fear he'll be famous no matter what," Will said.

"Icho is certainly making big of it in the *Chronicle*," Valerie explained. "But he earned something out of it."

"Anyway, Val," Charlie said, "I think you did the right thing."

Valerie didn't respond to this right away. She questioned it, and she would continue to question it. She didn't know for sure that Eric Grant was going to kill Will. She guessed. An educated guess, but was that worth the man's life, no matter how evil he was?

Valerie was uncertain. She never could stomach taking a life. But she did what she did, and all she knew was that Will was alive. That was what she would hold onto.

Finally, she answered her friend.

"Thanks, Charlie. How is the family?"

"Fine," Charlie said. "They're just happy I've got a couple of weeks off work now. But I'm stuck out the back building a tree house. It's far more frustrating than our cases."

Valerie patted him on the arm and then gave Will a hug.

"I'll see you in two days, okay?" she said.

"I see I'm the only one committed to come around here every day," Charlie said, sitting down.

"Tom has invited me to see his family."

"Ooh," Charlie said. "That's a power move. Once you see the family, that's it, you're part of their tribe... if they like you." He grinned. "You haven't got anything to worry about, Val."

"I hope not," she sighed. She was worried that they'd ask about her family. And then what would she tell them? *Oh, my sister and mother are in psychiatric wards and my father abandoned me.*

"And Valerie, remember what I said earlier," Will said, looking tired. "It's never too late to go searching."

Valerie smiled. "See ya, guys."

She headed out of the hospital. But as she wandered through the brightly lit halls and then out into the cool air, she gripped her phone in her hand.

Will had nearly died. That had shaken Valerie. Life was short. She had to know about the message her mom had sent.

Valerie dialed a number in her phone.

"Hello?" a man's voice said.

"Hey, Jackson. I know it's your day off."

"Hi, Agent Law, what can I do for you?"

"I need your help. I want to find my father."

NOW AVAILABLE!

NO FEAR
(A Valerie Law FBI Suspense Thriller—Book 3)

From #1 bestselling mystery and suspense author Blake Pierce comes book #3 in a gripping new series: the FBI's elite new unit targeting criminally-insane killers is summoned when a series of murders occurs that bears the signature of a psychotic killer. But something bothers FBI Special Agent Valerie Law about this case: this killer, she fears, may just be more normal than anyone suspects.

"A masterpiece of thriller and mystery."
—Books and Movie Reviews, Roberto Mattos (re *Once Gone*)

NO FEAR is book #3 in a new series by #1 bestselling mystery and suspense author Blake Pierce.

Faced with an unpredictable killer and a lack of information, Valerie must use her brilliant mind to connect the dots—and fast. Her only hope of catching him is to work backwards, and to delve into his past.

Will she crack the killer's code in time to save the next victim?

Or will she be too late?

A page-turning crime thriller featuring a brilliant and haunted new female protagonist, the VALERIE LAW mystery series is packed with suspense and driven by a breakneck pace that will keep you turning pages late into the night.

Books #4-#6 are also available!

"An edge of your seat thriller in a new series that keeps you turning pages! ...So many twists, turns and red herrings... I can't wait to see what happens next."
—Reader review (*Her Last Wish*)

"A strong, complex story about two FBI agents trying to stop a serial killer. If you want an author to capture your attention and have you guessing, yet trying to put the pieces together, Pierce is your author!"
—Reader review (*Her Last Wish*)

"A typical Blake Pierce twisting, turning, roller coaster ride suspense thriller. Will have you turning the pages to the last sentence of the last chapter!!!"
—Reader review (*City of Prey*)

"Right from the start we have an unusual protagonist that I haven't seen done in this genre before. The action is nonstop... A very atmospheric novel that will keep you turning pages well into the wee hours."
—Reader review (*City of Prey*)

"Everything that I look for in a book... a great plot, interesting characters, and grabs your interest right away. The book moves along at a breakneck pace and stays that way until the end. Now on go I to book two!"
—Reader review (*Girl, Alone*)

"Exciting, heart pounding, edge of your seat book... a must read for mystery and suspense readers!"
—Reader review (*Girl, Alone*)

Blake Pierce

Blake Pierce is the USA Today bestselling author of the RILEY PAGE mystery series, which includes seventeen books. Blake Pierce is also the author of the MACKENZIE WHITE mystery series, comprising fourteen books; of the AVERY BLACK mystery series, comprising six books; of the KERI LOCKE mystery series, comprising five books; of the MAKING OF RILEY PAIGE mystery series, comprising six books; of the KATE WISE mystery series, comprising seven books; of the CHLOE FINE psychological suspense mystery, comprising six books; of the JESSE HUNT psychological suspense thriller series, comprising twenty four books; of the AU PAIR psychological suspense thriller series, comprising three books; of the ZOE PRIME mystery series, comprising six books; of the ADELE SHARP mystery series, comprising fifteen books, of the EUROPEAN VOYAGE cozy mystery series, comprising four books; of the new LAURA FROST FBI suspense thriller, comprising nine books (and counting); of the new ELLA DARK FBI suspense thriller, comprising eleven books (and counting); of the A YEAR IN EUROPE cozy mystery series, comprising nine books, of the AVA GOLD mystery series, comprising six books (and counting); of the RACHEL GIFT mystery series, comprising six books (and counting); of the VALERIE LAW mystery series, comprising six books (and counting); of the PAIGE KING mystery series, comprising six books (and counting); and of the MAY MOORE mystery series, comprising three books (and counting).

An avid reader and lifelong fan of the mystery and thriller genres, Blake loves to hear from you, so please feel free to visit www.blakepierceauthor.com to learn more and stay in touch.

BOOKS BY BLAKE PIERCE

MAY MOORE MYSTERY SERIES
NEVER RUN (Book #1)
NEVER TELL (Book #2)
NEVER LIVE (Book #3)

PAIGE KING MYSTERY SERIES
THE GIRL HE PINED (Book #1)
THE GIRL HE CHOSE (Book #2)
THE GIRL HE TOOK (Book #3)
THE GIRL HE WISHED (Book #4)
THE GIRL HE CROWNED (Book #5)
THE GIRL HE WATCHED (Book #6)

VALERIE LAW MYSTERY SERIES
NO MERCY (Book #1)
NO PITY (Book #2)
NO FEAR (Book #3)
NO SLEEP (Book #4)
NO QUARTER (Book #5)
NO CHANCE (Book #6)

RACHEL GIFT MYSTERY SERIES
HER LAST WISH (Book #1)
HER LAST CHANCE (Book #2)
HER LAST HOPE (Book #3)
HER LAST FEAR (Book #4)
HER LAST CHOICE (Book #5)
HER LAST BREATH (Book #6)

AVA GOLD MYSTERY SERIES
CITY OF PREY (Book #1)
CITY OF FEAR (Book #2)
CITY OF BONES (Book #3)
CITY OF GHOSTS (Book #4)
CITY OF DEATH (Book #5)

CITY OF VICE (Book #6)

A YEAR IN EUROPE
A MURDER IN PARIS (Book #1)
DEATH IN FLORENCE (Book #2)
VENGEANCE IN VIENNA (Book #3)
A FATALITY IN SPAIN (Book #4)

ELLA DARK FBI SUSPENSE THRILLER
GIRL, ALONE (Book #1)
GIRL, TAKEN (Book #2)
GIRL, HUNTED (Book #3)
GIRL, SILENCED (Book #4)
GIRL, VANISHED (Book 5)
GIRL ERASED (Book #6)
GIRL, FORSAKEN (Book #7)
GIRL, TRAPPED (Book #8)
GIRL, EXPENDABLE (Book #9)
GIRL, ESCAPED (Book #10)
GIRL, HIS (Book #11)

LAURA FROST FBI SUSPENSE THRILLER
ALREADY GONE (Book #1)
ALREADY SEEN (Book #2)
ALREADY TRAPPED (Book #3)
ALREADY MISSING (Book #4)
ALREADY DEAD (Book #5)
ALREADY TAKEN (Book #6)
ALREADY CHOSEN (Book #7)
ALREADY LOST (Book #8)
ALREADY HIS (Book #9)

EUROPEAN VOYAGE COZY MYSTERY SERIES
MURDER (AND BAKLAVA) (Book #1)
DEATH (AND APPLE STRUDEL) (Book #2)
CRIME (AND LAGER) (Book #3)
MISFORTUNE (AND GOUDA) (Book #4)
CALAMITY (AND A DANISH) (Book #5)
MAYHEM (AND HERRING) (Book #6)

ADELE SHARP MYSTERY SERIES
LEFT TO DIE (Book #1)
LEFT TO RUN (Book #2)
LEFT TO HIDE (Book #3)
LEFT TO KILL (Book #4)
LEFT TO MURDER (Book #5)
LEFT TO ENVY (Book #6)
LEFT TO LAPSE (Book #7)
LEFT TO VANISH (Book #8)
LEFT TO HUNT (Book #9)
LEFT TO FEAR (Book #10)
LEFT TO PREY (Book #11)
LEFT TO LURE (Book #12)
LEFT TO CRAVE (Book #13)
LEFT TO LOATHE (Book #14)
LEFT TO HARM (Book #15)

THE AU PAIR SERIES
ALMOST GONE (Book#1)
ALMOST LOST (Book #2)
ALMOST DEAD (Book #3)

ZOE PRIME MYSTERY SERIES
FACE OF DEATH (Book#1)
FACE OF MURDER (Book #2)
FACE OF FEAR (Book #3)
FACE OF MADNESS (Book #4)
FACE OF FURY (Book #5)
FACE OF DARKNESS (Book #6)

A JESSIE HUNT PSYCHOLOGICAL SUSPENSE SERIES
THE PERFECT WIFE (Book #1)
THE PERFECT BLOCK (Book #2)
THE PERFECT HOUSE (Book #3)
THE PERFECT SMILE (Book #4)
THE PERFECT LIE (Book #5)
THE PERFECT LOOK (Book #6)
THE PERFECT AFFAIR (Book #7)

THE PERFECT ALIBI (Book #8)
THE PERFECT NEIGHBOR (Book #9)
THE PERFECT DISGUISE (Book #10)
THE PERFECT SECRET (Book #11)
THE PERFECT FAÇADE (Book #12)
THE PERFECT IMPRESSION (Book #13)
THE PERFECT DECEIT (Book #14)
THE PERFECT MISTRESS (Book #15)
THE PERFECT IMAGE (Book #16)
THE PERFECT VEIL (Book #17)
THE PERFECT INDISCRETION (Book #18)
THE PERFECT RUMOR (Book #19)
THE PERFECT COUPLE (Book #20)
THE PERFECT MURDER (Book #21)
THE PERFECT HUSBAND (Book #22)
THE PERFECT SCANDAL (Book #23)
THE PERFECT MASK (Book #24)

CHLOE FINE PSYCHOLOGICAL SUSPENSE SERIES
NEXT DOOR (Book #1)
A NEIGHBOR'S LIE (Book #2)
CUL DE SAC (Book #3)
SILENT NEIGHBOR (Book #4)
HOMECOMING (Book #5)
TINTED WINDOWS (Book #6)

KATE WISE MYSTERY SERIES
IF SHE KNEW (Book #1)
IF SHE SAW (Book #2)
IF SHE RAN (Book #3)
IF SHE HID (Book #4)
IF SHE FLED (Book #5)
IF SHE FEARED (Book #6)
IF SHE HEARD (Book #7)

THE MAKING OF RILEY PAIGE SERIES
WATCHING (Book #1)
WAITING (Book #2)

LURING (Book #3)
TAKING (Book #4)
STALKING (Book #5)
KILLING (Book #6)

RILEY PAIGE MYSTERY SERIES
ONCE GONE (Book #1)
ONCE TAKEN (Book #2)
ONCE CRAVED (Book #3)
ONCE LURED (Book #4)
ONCE HUNTED (Book #5)
ONCE PINED (Book #6)
ONCE FORSAKEN (Book #7)
ONCE COLD (Book #8)
ONCE STALKED (Book #9)
ONCE LOST (Book #10)
ONCE BURIED (Book #11)
ONCE BOUND (Book #12)
ONCE TRAPPED (Book #13)
ONCE DORMANT (Book #14)
ONCE SHUNNED (Book #15)
ONCE MISSED (Book #16)
ONCE CHOSEN (Book #17)

MACKENZIE WHITE MYSTERY SERIES
BEFORE HE KILLS (Book #1)
BEFORE HE SEES (Book #2)
BEFORE HE COVETS (Book #3)
BEFORE HE TAKES (Book #4)
BEFORE HE NEEDS (Book #5)
BEFORE HE FEELS (Book #6)
BEFORE HE SINS (Book #7)
BEFORE HE HUNTS (Book #8)
BEFORE HE PREYS (Book #9)
BEFORE HE LONGS (Book #10)
BEFORE HE LAPSES (Book #11)
BEFORE HE ENVIES (Book #12)
BEFORE HE STALKS (Book #13)
BEFORE HE HARMS (Book #14)

Printed in the USA
CPSIA information can be obtained
at www.ICGtesting.com
LVHW040604060624
782431LV00003B/228

9 781094 376868